Signs of Silence

Book 2
in the series with
My Hands Have Something To Say
Dorey Rasmussen

ISBN-10: 1530712726

ISBN:9798224285877

A day when deaf people and their language are completely accepted—no, more than that, truly welcomed—as a part of the family of man, in which God created diversity not to oppress the minority who are different, but to enrich the lives of all.
Laurent Clerc

ACKNOWLEDGMENTS

. . . .

To my sister from another mother, Mindy Diaz for pushing me and encouraging me all the way. My sisters, Linda and Jennifer for their support in both spoken words and signed. And my husband for telling me, "Yes you can!" Finally, to AJ and Haylee for cheerfully exclaiming, "you're an author!"

CHAPTER 1 December 1941

. . . .

Richard Moeller was sitting in his barracks listening to the rain falling outside. The raindrops sounded like rocks hitting the metal roof as it had all day during the summer storm. His cot covered with the standard green, wool blanket was hard compared to his bed at home where he grew up on Martha's Vineyard. Most of the newly enlisted were either sleeping in their bunks, off in the recreation area, listening to the radio, or writing letters home. Life at Fort Lee wasn't anything reminiscent of the life Richard was used to in college.

Each morning started at 0500 when the sound of reveille broke the quiet of the night. The troops filed into the mess hall for breakfast and then out for calisthenics. Their march took them through the woods, wading through creeks, up and down the difficult terrain in the afternoon heat of Virginia, cooled by the rain. They had very little time to appreciate the scenery. Heavy packs weighed down on their backs; half the troop carried rifles on the first section of the hike while the others carried them back on the return trip. Equipment was scarce, there were not enough rifles for each of them to carry their own yet, more would be issued later. The obstacle courses were just as demanding as the cross-country excursions; running through the course, crawling under barbed wire rolls through the muddy pits, climbing down landing nets then thrusting and parrying with bayonets fixed to the end of a rifle. The soldiers would collapse from exhaustion in the barrack with sweat soaking their uniforms.

It has been six months since the attack on Pearl Harbor. Richard made the decision to join the service immediately after graduation, five months after the brutal assault on the American fleet. The unimaginable day was emblazoned in his mind forever. He was in the student lounge studying for exams that Sunday morning eager for

Christmas break to arrive when someone turned up the radio and a crowd gathered around the desk. He had been absently following the New York Giants and Brooklyn Dodgers football game in the background.

He remembers the looks of disbelief and concern for friends and family stationed on the island. Some spouted racial slurs vowing revenge, others sought out the closest phone.

"My brother is over there. He is on the Arizona," the young man stood frozen listening to the reports.

Richard had stood staring at the wooden box which delivered the news thrusting them all into a war they now knew was inevitable.

"From the newsroom in New York, President Roosevelt said in a statement today that the Japanese have attacked Pearl Harbor from the air."

The reports had been sporadic; the loss of life mounted with each report. News eventually came of the USS Arizona's demise and the insinuation of thousands of servicemen. Another frenzy of activity had erupted in the room when rumors of additional attacks on the California coast were broadcast on the radio which fortunately turned out to be false. A forgotten pencil was the only thing that moved in the room when it rolled off the table and onto the floor breaking the implacable silence.

Richard had gathered his books and ran across the courtyard to his dorm where there was already a line for the only phone in the hall when he walked through the door. He bent over to catch his breath.

"Are you going to enlist?" Gerald Johnson had asked Richard as he burst through the door.

They had been roommates for three years and both would be graduating in a few months. He was the same height as Richard and the same dark hair. Richard was heavier set with a muscular build from years of swimming in the surf. But both men were very popular with the girls in town, going to various clubs or the frequent party on campus. Gerald was waiting to call home, standing there in his grey trousers and round-necked sweater.

"Several of the other fellows were discussing going into town to the post office to enlist right away into the service," Gerald continued and pushed his glasses back up on his nose. There was a wide range of emotions among them.

"Where is Pearl Harbor," someone asked. Thomas Harding stood off by himself, inside he was torn between wanting to join his friends to defend his country and his strong belief against war and killing for any reason. He knew seeking a Conscientious Objector status would be frowned upon.

"I don't know," Richard answered Gerald's question about enlisting. "I need to talk to my dad. I'm thinking about driving home, but I don't want to miss classes tomorrow."

Richard's parents lived in the house he was born in on Martha's Vineyard in Oak Bluffs. It would only take him a few hours from campus. Richard was studying business and finance; his dream was to eventually work on Wall Street. Numbers intrigued him; he looked at numbers differently from others. When looking at a problem, he could already see the answer in his mind.

"Jeeze, they sank our fleet!" Someone else ran into the room, "did you hear? Pearl Harbor was attacked by Japan!"

"My brother is a doctor and stationed out there," another added. "What a mess, I thought we could stay out of the damn war."

"I can only imagine the scene on the Hawaiian Islands, there are thousands of sailors on the battleships and countless other vessels. The radio announcer said there were fires erupting on the water due to the gas and oil streaming from the ships. The California, Arizona, and West Virginia all sunk and the Oklahoma capsized." Richard was not even aware that so many ships were docked in Hawaii, but the Japanese were.

"This is awful," Gerald added.

Richard looked at his watch while standing in line for the phone in his brown wool pants, white collar shirt and green sweater vest. It was nearly 4 o'clock; he decided to wait to drive home and to call as soon as he could get a chance at the phone.

In May of 1942, Richard Moeller graduated from Harvard. His parents sat in the crowd bursting with pride for their son and everything he had already accomplished in his short 23 years. Richard found his parents waiting for him outside the hall after the ceremony. Timothy Moeller knew what his son had planned for the afternoon. The two men had several conversations in the past few months following the uncertain times the United States was feeling.

The U.S. entered the war immediately in December; by January the first American forces had already reached Great Britain. The draft had been extended in 1941. As far as Richard was concerned, a career could wait until after his service. He was allowed to finish school which many of his friends chose not to do when they enlisted immediately. Richard and his parents drove together to the enlistment office where Timothy and Annette Moeller watched their son sign his commitment to his country. Richard was trading his graduation gown for an Army uniform, his pencils for a gun. He would go through a physical and leave for training the following day.

Richard's mom dabbed at her eyes with her cotton handkerchief as she watched her son pass through the doors with the other enlistees prepared to defend their country. Just hours before Annette had watched him walk through the auditorium and receive his diploma, so much was changing so quickly. Mrs. Moeller clung to the small white service flag with a blue star, she would be hanging the in the front window designating that there was a family member in the service.

"If your son is sent overseas which was very likely, the star would be changed to silver." Annette listened to their instructions as the waited, but she didn't want to think about the gold stars she had already seen since war was declared.

They had so many memories of their son, and the two parents looked forward to many more with him when he returned from the war, if they were so fortunate. Richard's decision to finish school and get his degree assisted him in getting into Officer's school, but first he had several months of training ahead of him.

By late July, Richard had already completed his eight weeks of basic training reduced from 14 weeks after the United States' entry into WWII. He endured four weeks of drills and was at the tail end of his Special Quartermaster training at Camp Lee. Next, he would enter Officer training before shipping out to where ever he was assigned. He was writing to his parents after another tough day and had a class to attend after dinner. His typical schedule had consisted of training, lectures, and trying to catch some sleep. Richard told his father about the lecture of War and It's Causes, and how this one started. He watched a film about the Article of War and Safeguarding Military Information. There was another lecture on chemical warfare all while attending more classes Monday, Tuesday and Thursday nights. He estimated 1200 men in the Battalion. There were four platoons in the company, four companies in the battalion and two battalions in the regiment. Camp Lee encompassed four regiments of men coming in for training and shipping out just as quickly as a new platoon arrived at the camp.

"You had better speed it up. We have to scram in a few minutes," Matthew Benton rubbed his hair with a towel having just come from the showers.

He was Richard's closest friend since they both arrived in Virginia. They shared letters from home with each other and went into a local joint in town whenever they were given leave. Most nights, lights out came at 11 p.m. with the exception of Saturday unless the Drill Sergeant made other plans for the platoon. They were both attending classes for officer classification. Matthew was from West Tisbury; the two never met before arriving in Virginia even though they lived so close to each other for so long. They felt a common bond as soon as they started talking in the barracks about life on the island, school, girls; nothing was left untouched. Richard quickly understood the expression of brotherhood; these are the men that his life could depend on one day.

Army life wasn't what he expected; however, most wouldn't have known what to expect. The men found that they had little time to do anything other than the training, preparing the soldiers for the duty they would carry out when the time came.

"I'm almost finished. I needed to catch up on a couple of letters. I think the mailroom holds onto our letters until there is a pile, and then they deliver them. I've got three letters I have to answer."

"That's swell, I haven't had a single letter in weeks. Dad is so busy on the farm since I left, he doesn't write much." Matthew tossed his towel on the top bunk, pulled his (GI) Government Issue slacks and shirt out his locker; he didn't want to be late for chow.

"Let's scoot." Richard folded the paper he was writing on, and put the letter in an envelope. He would drop it off to be mailed on their way to the mess hall. "At least your pop doesn't have to worry about the rationing; your family has all the beef you can handle."

"He is trying to get a government contract. He would really be the Big Cheese if he could work that out. We were selling off the sheep so we could buy more cattle and plant more corn and potatoes." Matthew and Richard left the barracks and walked up the short wood plank ramp to the dirt road. Each company had its own street leading to the mess hall and administrative buildings.

"He could send some of that here to us. Some of these meals have been unrecognizable. You have to be hard boiled to stomach some of this food." Richard thought of his mother's cooking as they walked down the dirt path kicking up the dust with each step.

"Just wait until we are in the trenches, you'll wish you had some of this grub." Matthew teased Richard as they walked through the screened door, each of them picked up a tray and started moving through the line.

The simple framed, wood building was able to hold hundreds of hungry men at the same time. They walked along the wood floor carrying their trays of food, and sat at a table on the far side of the room. They only had a little time before their class would start.

"Maybe they could bring our mothers down here to cook." Richard poked at the pork chop on his tray then scooped his peas over into his mashed potatoes. Richard's mother told their friends countless times that he was a born leader. They were thrilled when he announced his acceptance into Office Training in his last letter. He had been President of his class in High School; he was often the person his friends turned to for advice. He played the piano in school for the choir and in church as well when they needed someone to sit in.

During their down time at Camp Lee, Richard could be found in the recreation room pounding out a tune of the old upright piano sitting in the corner. Several of the soldiers would make requests while the group would stand singing to the tune Richard offered.

"I'm done here. We're going to be late?" Richard deposited his tray with the stack sitting on the cart as they headed out the door.

"Tonight's class is about teambuilding," the instructor began, typical of the subjects they would study. "The purpose of the training you are receiving is to instill standards of conduct, leadership, and military knowledge to perform the skills that will be expected of you."

Richard jotted some notes as the trainer lectured to the officer candidates. He hoped that the training he received would help him in the future after the war. He knew he would return to the East Coast; hopefully, getting a position dealing with stocks.

"I'm beat," he told Matthew on their way back to the barracks. "I didn't get much sleep and expected that it will only get worse once we ship out."

Only days later, their Commanding officer gathered the company and announced they would in fact be shipping out. There had been rumors for weeks that their fate was getting closer.

"Gather your duffle bags and packs and report to the transportation area. Move out!"

"Good bye rain, good bye mosquitoes." Richard stood with Matthew and the other men of their platoon waiting to board one of the many canvas covered trucks.

The group arrived at the train station by early afternoon; there were crowds of civilians wishing them a safe trip, flags waving and salutes from veterans and a small boy who stood out off the curb. The movement of troops was a site not unfamiliar to the residents of the area.

"I have not been on a train since traveling with my parents to upstate New York to visit relatives." He was used to the velvet covered seats in the cars they would travel in. He stood on the platform as another train rumbled out of the station; he could smell oil, and feel the vibration of the powerful engines under his feet.

Steam rose from under the train rising from the rails as he stepped up the metal stairs into the train. The seats were wooden slats and worn from years of use.

"We are going to New Jersey where we will board another train for the west coast." He told Matthew after overhearing the news. Richard had been able to get a quick cable out to his parents hoping they could drive north so he could see them. Gas rationing made long trips difficult, but he hoped his father would figure out a way to get up there.

The train finally slowed as it rolled into the station after hours of swaying on the tracks and the rhythmic clacking from metal riding over metal. Heat rolled down the aisle of the car where most of the soldiers were asleep huddled against the window or hunched over with their bag on their lap for something to lay their head on.

It was nearly midnight when several officers walked down the aisle of the cars. "Grab your gear, let's go. Move it, move it, move it!"

Richard shook the stiffness from his body as he stood up and grabbed his bags and shuffled to the rear of the car they had been riding in and stepped down to the dark station.

"Fall in," Captain Franks yelled. The men lined up by platoon as commanded and began the march down the streets.

"We are in Atlantic City," Matthew recognized the scenery as they marched in unison. "I've been down these streets before during better times." He flipped the strap on his duffle back up on his shoulder and stepped on the moon reflecting off the puddles of water.

Now the streets were quiet and damp serving as a path for the young men headed to war.

"I saw the sign when we pulled in. I wish I could get word to my dad exactly where we are going." Richard whispered as he adjusted his backpack keeping stride with the others. Little did he know, Timothy Moeller was waiting at the station when they arrived and had inquired as to how long they would be there and where the troops were going to stay for the night.

"This is the Ritz. It used to be a pretty swanky place." Matthew was excited for no reason in particular; most likely he was looking forward to a decent place to sleep. As they assembled in front of the building and counted off, they were assigned six to a room for the night.

"Get some sleep gentlemen, this isn't a party. No dames, no hooch, bed down and get ready for 0600 reveille." The captain looked tired, but wasn't about to show it or disclose to the men their destination.

Richard spotted his father standing just inside the door as he entered the building. "Applesauce! I'll be up in a few minutes," expressing his excitement he told Matthew who would be sharing a room with him. "Hello, sir."

"You look well son; the army has been good to you." Timothy shook his son's hand and pulled him in to a hug. His son's shoulders were a little broader and more muscular. He missed his son and did not tell Annette how worried he was for Richard. "I know you have to report to your room, but when we got your telegram, I wanted to get up here to see you off. I had to call in a few favors to find your whereabouts."

"Thanks pop. How's mom?" Richard wanted to hold onto the moment forever. He didn't know if he would ever see the man who raised him ever again.

"She sends her love. She has been helping with the Red Cross rolling bandages, and putting together care packages for the men overseas." Timothy noticed that Richard was studying his face and imagined what he was thinking and how scared those boys must be.

"Give her a hug for me." Richard glanced over at his CO who eyeballed him for disobeying orders. Deep inside he was envious that the soldier's father had made the trip to see his son and wished his own father had been able to be there. These were stressful times for everyone with loved ones scattered all over the world in horrendous situations.

"Mother has your star hanging in the window, we are very proud of you son." Timothy handed his son a bag with some baked goods from his mother and a few cartons of cigarettes he managed to save with his rations and others donated by their friends. "You take care of yourself and write as often as you can."

"I will dad." Richard felt like he was going off to college again, leaving his home and the family he loved. He was embarking on a journey that would forever change his life. Father and son exchanged another hug before Richard picked up his gear and followed the line up the stairs to his room.

Timothy watched his son disappear as Richard rounded the corner, and climbed several flights of stairs. He gave a quick look over to Richard's CO who nodded in his direction. Mr. Moeller gave a quick salute and excused himself as he exited past the soldiers who continued to file into the building. He himself had served in the Great War. He was fortunate to escape any serious wounds and made it home able to start a family with the woman who waited for him. Timothy was well aware of the dangers Richard faced.

Richard walked to the far end of the hall which was covered with red carpet and found his room number. The walls were bare; all of the artwork had been removed. He opened the door to the once extravagant room to two bunks and two cots assembled in the room with a large dresser and a small bathroom. All of the other furnishings had been removed from the rooms to house as many soldiers as possible. Richard thought they could have left a few things to make them more comfortable, but in retrospect, it was a stepping stone to the fields and trenches they would be living in soon.

"So where do you think we are headed?" Anderson asked from the top of his bunk. The feet of the 6'2" soldier were hanging over the end; he said it was more comfortable than the bottom bunk.

"I have heard England, Italy, even Greenland. I guess we will know when we get there." Matthew thought of the reels they had watched at the theater showing the German air attacks on Stalingrad and Rommel's advances. There were films of American soldiers enjoying the European countryside; an obvious tactic to get more men to enlist. They had heard plenty of horrific stories while training at Camp Lee.

"You know," Gibson tossed his boots on the floor with a loud 'thump'. "I should have signed up to be a pilot. Up there in the sky, home every night to a warm bed and food. Those high hats have it made."

"Except when they get shot, they fall a couple thousand feet instead of a few feet. That's the flattest theory I've ever heard." Richard threw his shirt at Gibson and laid back on the cot that Matthew had saved for him.

"Moeller, I heard that was your old man in the lobby... you some bluenose? How did you set that up?"

"I sent him a cable when I heard we were shipping out of Lee. He's a smart man, figured out where we were headed."

"I'd like to see my old man," Anderson answered from above them. "He was upset when I decided to sign up. My little sis thinks I look pretty keen in my uniform."

"How old is your sister?"

"Don't even think about it, she's seventeen and not some dame for you lamebrains."

"Too bad we can't stay for a few nights. I'd like to find me some gams to do what I'm thinking about." Reynolds said while dreaming of a pair of long, bare legs.

He was the fifth in the room, lying on the other bunk. They had all been in Officer's Training together, ironically, they were assigned to room together. He was the rowdiest of the group, but he was smart and probably the savviest when they studied combat tactics. Everyone could see the rough exterior he showed, it was the fear inside that he kept bottled up. Reynolds' girl dumped him right after he signed up for the army. She opted for some college stiff that was not eligible for enlistment for a supposed medical condition. He drank a lot for a week after receiving the letter until his buddies helped him pull out of his depression, they were afraid that he may get kicked out of officer training.

Sherrott was already snoring, lying on top of the blanket stretched on the bed. He never even took his boots off.

"Turn out the lights, we only have a few hours before we're back on our feet." Richard pulled the pillow from behind his head and covered his ears so he could at least get a couple hours of sleep.

The troops boarded another train the next morning. The old Pullman cars were filled with soldiers before pulling out. They went up to New York, added more cars to the line loaded with more soldiers and headed west. They still did not know where their final destination, everyone was still speculating on the rumors each of them had heard.

One of the cars had been converted into a mess hall, preparing the food that was served through the eighteen cars of soldiers trying to occupy themselves and not think about the war they were headed full steam into. Two days of listening to the clicking of the wheels riding over the tracks and swaying from side to side they crossed the Ohio border and the train finally started to slow down. Several of the men stood up to look out the windows to see where they were. The fields were being harvested while others were dotted with cattle grazing on the uncut grass.

"Looks a lot like home doesn't it," Moeller said turning his head to look at Benton sitting beside him.

"Yeah, more or less. I bet you miss the water."

"We are going west; I have the feeling we are going to see more water than I care to see."

"Looks that way." Matthew sat up in his seat to get a better look at the landscape. "I wonder why we are slowing down." They could see a few buildings in the distance, other than that, there were fields on both sides of the tracks.

Eventually, the train came to a stop in what looked like a make-shift town. It was small, but there were a lot of people greeting them as they pulled in.

"Dennison Depot, I've heard about this place." Richard looked around to see if there was any activity in the forward cars. He knew the COs were in the more comfortable cars for the long trip. He could see a few silos, as well as, several houses. As they shuffled down the aisle to the end of the car, Richard looked at the red brick building. The eave ran the entire length of the station under dormers with stained glass windows. It was a nice place seemingly in the middle of nowhere. He stepped off the train and stretched, still feeling the sensation of the moving train under his feet.

They were greeted by a sign, 'The Salvation Army Canteen'. Matthew and Richard followed the other men lining up into the canteen where they were served hot coffee and sandwiches. There were several women, most likely locals from the area serving the soldiers.

"This is very kind of you ma'am," Richard expressed to the woman his mother's age who handed him a cup that she had just poured.

"You just promise to keep yourself safe and get back to your loved ones as quickly as possible." She had a rhythmic accent not like the ones they had grown familiar with when in Virginia.

"They call this place Dreamsville. I believe that, did you see that girl?" Reynolds was at it again. He had a one-track mind.

"I think her mother would take a pitch fork to your hide if you made a move." They all laughed.

Richard took two sandwiches and walked back outside to breath in some of the fresh air. It was nice to get off the train and smell the Ohio breeze as it blew softly past them. He had to admit that it was much better than the smell of hundreds of soldiers in their cotton khaki shirts and trousers, ankle length russet leather service shoes and Olive Drab canvas leggings. Some of the men wore their OD cotton field jacket and others left them on the train. There was a nice breeze, but it was still hot outside. Richard had loosened his tie on the train, but cinched it back up before entering the canteen.

They walked around the station and found a grassy area where they could stretch out. Richard was enjoying the rays of sun; he finished a cigarette and was just beginning to doze off when he heard the order to fall in. The men groaned while rising to their feet and hurried back to the train. Loading back onto the train did not take long and soon they were moving again.

"Who's up for a game of gin?" Gibson pulled a deck of cards out of his duffle and started shuffling the cards. A few of the guys faced each other in the aisle as hands were dealt to each of them.

The men were in good spirits after the stop, some were singing, playing cards while others moved to the sleeping cabins which they rotated in and out of. Within a week they pulled into the Naval Base of

San Diego and again they marched to the barracks that they would stay in for the remainder of their training until shipping out - again.

• • • •

September 1942. The troops were paraded for the visiting brass. The Company marched past the platform and saluted the Colonel and Major General who would command the division. The band played as the soldiers marched through the field and stood at attention. Richard was thankful that a cool breeze was coming in off the Pacific Ocean. As the soldiers marched across the bare field, they left a trail of dust floating in the air. There were stark differences in the area with cool, lush valleys, inviting beaches and barren fields. The new officers were presented their promotions during the ceremony. Richard was now a 2nd Lieutenant, as well as Matthew Benton and the other men who were in his class. The troops were given the "fall out" command and retreated for the R & R that was granted. The newly promoted Lieutenants headed into town to celebrate. They jumped onto the streetcar looking for a gin mill and some dancing. They found plenty of both.

The men walked the streets of the Gas lamp Quarter they had heard so much about, touting the new yellow bar on their uniforms. Richard looked up at the buildings; they were nothing like those in New York and Boston he had grown so accustom to. There was such a mix of cultures in the architecture. He wasn't an expert, but he and the others noticed the influences and examples of the various Victorian styles. He liked the Spanish Renaissance Revival and the Italian Baroque Revival the most. The detailing in the stained-glass windows, carvings, and columns in such vibrant colors seemed to mesmerize him. He imagined a young bride standing on the balcony looking out to sea waiting for her soldier to come home. Richard was sure there were plenty of those situations, some would have happy endings and unfortunately many would not.

"Where you at man?" Benton punched his arm shaking him back to the present.

"Just thinking about all those people at home worrying about what will happen to the guys overseas."

"You can't live in fear and do your job. Besides, we'll be home three shakes of a lamb's tail. Don't you worry."

"I'm not scared. Just thinking."

They rounded the corner standing in front of a building covered with large grey stone. Music streamed from the joint into the street. A few sailors slid past them going into the building. Richard noticed the sharp contrast of their white uniforms to the OD khakis his group wore.

"Sounds like this is the place," Anderson held the door open for the other fellas to follow his lead.

Reynolds was quick to bring over a couple of girls who had been sitting at a table alone. "Guys, this is Ann and Miss Hawkins," Reynolds introduced the girls to the group as he pulled up a couple of chairs for them.

"I moved to San Diego to help with the war movement, we both are secretaries on the shipyard," Ann informed them.

The men took turns dancing with the girls, Anderson was dancing to the <u>GI Jive</u> and then to the house band's rendition of the Andrew's Sisters song.

Richard politely bought a round of drinks when the girls returned to the table. He preferred to play the music rather than to dance to it. He wasn't planning on asking anyone to dance unless he felt obligated to do so. It wasn't long before Richard spotted the piano, and waited for the band to take a break. He got up from the table to do what would make him happy, sat down and fired up a song he had played at Camp Lee several times, _Waitin' for the Train to Come In_.

Surprisingly, Betsy Hawkins came over to the piano and started singing the Peggy Lee tune. Richard was impressed and smiled at her with approval. She had wavy shoulder length auburn hair, a long sexy neck, and plump lips covered with red lip rouge. The song was slow and reminiscent of the travels most of them had been through over the past few months and the anticipation of reuniting with girl friends in the future.

"I think I should pick up the tempo a bit. Do you know _Don't Sit Under the Apple Tree_?" he asked Betsy if she knew the song he had in mind. He felt so much at home sitting in front of the keys of the piano while Betsy belted it out.

The band returned to the small stage as Betsy finished the song and showed their appreciation. The crowd stopped dancing when the song ended and clapped for the duo. Several whistles reverberated in the room while Richard and Betsy walked back to the table as the group raised their glasses to them.

"I didn't know you could play like that," Gibson was impressed. "And you are quite the star," he said to Betsy moving closer to her. The band started to play again and the couples danced the jitterbug.

"Care to dance," Richard asked Betsy when she glanced at him as if asking him to save her from Gibson's grasp. He owed her that much after making him sound better than he really was.

"You have an incredible voice." She was wasting her time sitting in an office in his opinion. They rounded the dance floor with a swing to _Jukebox Saturday Night_.

He never had any siblings, but he felt close to this girl. He kept telling himself he had no desire to get involved with anyone right before shipping out for the war. So many soldiers had relationships that meant nothing to them other than someone to spend the night with. Richard wanted his relationships to mean something.

"You play very well; I enjoyed being able to sing with you. I'd really like to go to Hollywood, but for now I had to get a job to support myself." Betsy laughed while resting her hand on Richard's shoulder when the music turned slow again. "My father flipped when I said I was moving to California. I want to be a star." She tilted her head back and shook her hair while looking to the ceiling.

"I'm sure you will make it. You sing better than most in the movies now."

"I just love Judy Garland. She and Mickey Rooney are a scream. Do you watch the _Andy Hardy_ movies?"

"I used to wish I could play all those instruments he plays. He has so much energy. Maybe we could catch a movie while I'm here."

"That would be swell." Betsy liked the soldier and noticed her girlfriend was dancing much too close with Sherrott. Betsy rarely went out, but Ann had begged her to go tonight, she had 'no one else to go with her'.

The two new found friends walked back over to the table as the others eventually made their way back as well.

"Thanks for the dance. Cigarette?"

"No, thanks. I don't smoke."

"Bad habit I picked up in boot camp."

Anderson found yet another girl who joined the group and Sherrott got hold of a willing partner who joined them as well. Eventually, they pulled two tables together in order to accommodate the growing group.

"Andy and I are going to take the car out to the beach. Do you and your soldier want to come with us?" Ann leaned in to Betsy and tried to whisper the question. She didn't realize how loud she was actually speaking due to the amount of alcohol she had consumed.

Betsy gave Richard a concerned glance. He could see that she did not think it was a wise idea.

"You two go ahead. I will make sure Miss Hawkins gets home safely." Richard got up to talk to Sherrott and warned him in private to make sure Ann got home safe. Richard was ready to leave when he walked up to Betsy's side, it had been a long day for all of them. "We can leave anytime you want. We can get a cab and I'll drop you off on my way back to the base."

"That is very nice of you Richard, but I can get home fine."

"With all of these sailors around? Don't worry, I'll drop you off safely at home." Richard was a man of his word and had no intention of inviting himself in. As far as he was concerned, she was in safe hands with him. She was a great looking doll and all, but he reminded himself that he could not get involved. They stayed long enough to finish the Coca Cola they ordered. Richard was impressed when he offered her a drink and she opted for the cola. He finished his drink and held Betsy's chair as he stood behind her. "You cowboys stay out of trouble and lay off the hooch. I'll see you back on base."

"Horse feathers Moeller, don't be a party pooper!" Anderson was on a roll. Richard was worried about him going to the beach and possibly drowning, but he wasn't about to go and become a part of whatever trouble they were going to find.

"Be careful of that black water, it will swallow you up." He waved goodbye to the group. "Anyone want to share the cab?"

"We are going to hit the town all night, we'll see you later." Matthew was excited with the leave time they had and didn't want to sleep a minute of it away.

Richard walked beside Betsy as they left the building. He stepped to the curb and waved his hand in the air to the passing taxis until an empty vehicle finally pulled over to pick them up. "Would you like to get a cup of coffee before I drop you off?"

"That would be nice."

"The closest diner, please." Richard announced their request to the driver who pulled away from the curb into the flow of traffic, maneuvering a few blocks to a building which resembled a railroad car. The building was wider than most trains he had been on including the most recent one. He noticed the yellow painted steel and green roof as they climbed the steps. New steel construction was scarce these days while the U.S. was at war. Recent rationing brought the surge of gathering scrap for recycling.

The place was bright but inviting. The two found a table and Richard ordered two cups of coffee when the waiter came over in his white pants, shirt and jacket complete with a black bow tie to get their order. He preferred to work the day shift as the late-night patrons ordered little and the tips were slim. Richard watched him fill the cups for the soldiers sitting at the counter on the red vinyl covered stools. All of the benches at the tables were the same red material.

Richard played with the tattered menu with a _Royal Crown_ advertisement on the back while Betsy told him about her home back in Wisconsin. He told her all about Martha's Vineyard and the ocean. "I want to go see the beach while I'm here. Be able to say that I've had my feet in both oceans."

"I never saw an ocean before moving here," Betsy said. Richard found it hard to believe having grown up on the east coast surrounded by water all of his life.

"I love the beach and the waves crashing in. My friends and I would stand in the water and jump just as a wave would come up on us when we were kids. Most of the time we would take a boat out and sail around outside the harbor."

"Sounds dreamy, Wisconsin is such a drag. I had to get away from there and find myself out here."

Richard listened while she told him about the farms, the cows and her father making cheese for a living. He looked at the signs on the wall, "Breakfast All Day," and the Blue-Plate Special written on a chalk board that their waiter was changing for the patrons. They left the diner when they both had finished their coffee and hailed another cab. Betsy gave the driver the address to the apartment she shared with Ann. The driver navigated through the hills and delivered them to the address he had been given. Richard got out and politely offered her his hand while she climbed out of the cab behind him.

"I had a good evening, thank you for the coffee." Betsy had grown comfortable with Richard, but was not willing to invite him to come upstairs.

"Thank you for the conversation. It was nice to talk to someone not wearing the same olive drab uniform." They both laughed, putting her at ease again. "May I ring you? We could go see that movie I promised you."

"I would like that," she wrote down the number to the phone on the third-floor hallway. The women had to share not only the phone, but also the bathroom. It wasn't ideal, but Betsy was used to sharing a bathroom with her two sisters and brother back home.

Richard hopped into the cab and headed back to the base with a final wave from the back window.

The barracks were empty; most of the men were either still out on the town or left the city during their leave. He wished they had more time so he could see his parents, but he would need several weeks unless he flew home. Letters would take a long time to catch up with them, and probably longer once they shipped out. He pulled out some paper from his footlocker and wrote to his parents.

"Dear Mom and Pop,

It is now quarter past one (in the morning), I was thinking of you as I often do.

I have not received any letters lately it may take a while for the mail to catch up with us. No news yet where we are headed. I will get word out to you before we leave.

I went into town with the fellows tonight and had a few drinks. Yes, I even danced a little. I'm sure it was a hoot as I never could dance well. Met a nice girl from Wisconsin, she wants to be a movie star. Her father makes cheese and they have a good size farm with plenty of cattle. San Diego is very nice, I am hoping tomorrow I can find a beach and take to the water for a bit.

I received your note and the news clipping about Charlie. I'm sure his parents appreciate the support you have given them after their loss. Please send them my sympathy as well. We have heard many reports about the European fronts. I feel we will be going to the Pacific islands. Of course this is only speculation on my part.

Good news! I received my promotion to 2nd Lieutenant today. We were so hot standing in formation for hours with the dust blowing in our faces. I can still taste the dirt.

I will get new uniforms soon. We also received the new M1 Steel pots to replace the doughboys we have been wearing. The new helmets are bigger and will keep us from cracking our skulls. That was supposed to be funny mom, don't worry about me. My footlocker now consists of 2 pairs of shoes, plenty of underwear, socks and handkerchiefs. I have my summer and winter suits, an overcoat and raincoat, leggings, and caps. We eat out of a meal can and drink from canteens when we are in the field for maneuvers. I scratched my name into mine, they are hard to replace if you lose it. We each have a first aid kit, half a tent, haversack, cartridge belt and rifle. Imagine carrying all of this on your back, thankfully I am more fit than when I left home.

Thanks for the Chesterfields that you sent. I can get cigarettes at the PX however they are not the same. I am going to turn in although it is very quiet with so many staying in town for the night. We were up early and I am beat.

All my love,
Richard"

He folded the letter and tucked the paper away to mail in the morning. Richard dreamt that night about the island shore, the deep blue sky that met the equally brilliant water on the horizon. He was lying on his back in the small sail boat floating on the gentle waves. The sun was beating on his face. He could hear the birds calling to each other and the sound of the water playing a cadence on the side of his craft. Shielding his eyes from the sun streaming through the narrow window above him, Richard could hear the drills of a new platoon marching in the field when he woke.

Richard rolled out of bed and thought of Betsy and what a nice girl he thought she was. He picked up the pants he had left lying on the end of his bed and pulled her number from the pocket. After a shower and some chow, he went to the phone to ring her.

"May I speak with Miss Hawkins please," he asked the female voice who answered the phone. He held the line for several minutes.

"Hello?" Betsy was wrapped in her robe standing in the hall holding the receiver.

"Hi, Betsy, it's Richard. Moeller, we met last night. I hope that I am not calling too early. Were you up?" He asked.

"Hi Richard. I was doing some washing." She fibbed to him that she had only finally been able to get out of bed after a late night. Ann had not come home, so Betsy slept straight through the morning.

"I was wondering if you would like to catch that movie I promised if you are not too busy. We could catch a matinee and maybe some lunch. Have you seen _Star Spangled Rhythm_?"

"No."

Richard was disappointed by the response. He thought they got along swell the night before.

"I mean no, I have not seen that movie. I would love to go see the feature with you."

"Can you be ready in an hour?"

"I will be ready. Just ring when you get here." Betsy thought what a sight she must be standing there. She would have to make some quick repairs to her attire. She was used to the jeans and flannel shirts she would wear when helping her father on the farm. She never had to worry what she looked like, her hair pulled back in a pony tail and no makeup.

San Diego the woman paid more attention to what they looked like. Several of the girls meant to catch the eye of a sailor and perhaps marry before the men shipped out. They would go to the USO dances and to the YMCA where the soldiers hung out at. Betsy was more focused on making enough money to move to Hollywood and become an actress. The lush valley and harsh desert of Southern California was a sharp change from the prairies and Oak forests of her birthplace. She had loved wandering through those forests in the spring and summer months, standing so still the deer would walk right by her. Her father would take them to Lake Michigan for a family outing on a rare weekend. They would camp just beyond the shore at night and play in the water through the day.

Richard arrived right on the dot and rang the buzzer by the name "Hawkins" at the mailboxes in the wood paneled hallway. "It's Richard." He broadcast.

"I'll be right down." Betsy checked her hair and lipstick in the mirror. She decided against the last pair of stockings she had and had painted her legs instead. She would save the stocking for work or an evening date. She came to the door with a smile. "Thanks for calling, I have wanted to see this feature for weeks now."

"I haven't had much time to see a movie this year." They got into the cab that was waiting for them and Richard gave the driver the name of the theater. "I joined the Army the same day I graduated from college, so I have been pretty busy."

"That's pretty impressive, a Harvard man," She was worried about several of friends who also joined the service, many who were fighting overseas. None of them had Richard's education, but great soldiers just the same.

The two sat in their seats surrounded by several more service men and people from the area. The lights dimmed before going out and the Newsreel with music in the background came onto the screen preempting the film. Richard stared intently at the screen as the announcer described the scenes.

"MARINES HOLD FIRM IN SOLOMONS SOUTHERN PACIFIC—Reassuring pictures of goodly reinforcements of men and materiel for the Solomons area are seen leaving and arriving – while the boys on the spot continue to give a good account of themselves with plenty of prisoners to their credit. Mac ARTHUR'S MEN TAKE KOKODA NEW GUINEA—Australian fighters, under Gen. MacArthur, are keeping the Japs on the run in this wild jungle country. It's great to see how the native fuzzy-wuzzies recognize the United Nations fighters as their friends. GEN. HOLCOMB RE-PLEDGES MARINES WASHINGTON, D.C.—On 167th Anniversary of the Marine Corps, its Commandant, Lt. Gen. Thomas Holcomb re-pledges the Corps to the great tradition of unfaltering devotion to the Nation . . . and in promising Victory, he tells America that the Marines have just begun to fight. "NOW, LET'S WIN THE WAR"—DEWEY NEW YORK CITY—Gubernatorial victor, as New York goes Republican in a statewide landslide, Thomas E. Dewey calls on people to bury all factional differences. . . and unite in winning the war. HIGH SCHOOL WINS SCRAP CONTEST LOS ANGELES, CAL.—With 1450 students bringing in 180-tons of scrap metal, Belvedere Junior High School of Los Angeles takes first place in a drive in which every public school participated."

Sitting in the theater made Richard feel like he was home. He could close his eyes and picture the velvet chairs in the theater back on the island, propping his feet on the seat in front of him until the usher shone his flashlight on him and telling him to get his feet down. Richard and his friends would toss popcorn at one another until a man in the audience would tell them to 'shape up'. He laughed at the memory.

"What is so funny?" Betsy asked.

"I was thinking about going to the movie with my friends back home."

"Sounds like you have some swell friends." Betsy smiled at Richard. She enjoyed being with him even though they had just met.

"I got word that one of them was killed over in Europe. My parents and Charlie's are close. We grew up together." The Newsreel reminded Richard of his friend and the potential to lose many more of those he was close to.

"I'm so sorry, Richard." Betsy laid a hand on his arm to comfort him. "We can leave if you don't feel up to watching the movie."

"No, don't even think about leaving. I will be fine," he said. Richard sat back in his seat and offered Betsy the popcorn he was holding between them.

"Don't you just love Bob Hope? I think Dorothy Lamour sings just beautifully." Betsy was so full of energy. Richard tried to picture her starring with some of the big Hollywood headliners.

"When you make it big can I tell everyone that I knew you when?"

"We can stay friends and you introduce me to all your friends."

"Agreed." The elder couple behind Richard and Betsy asked them to quit talking so they could enjoy the film. Betsy giggled quietly and turned to the screen.

It was a wonderful day. After the movie, Richard took her out to lunch. That evening they went to the USO dance, she was a wonderful dancer. Richard felt bad that he had two left feet and had a difficult time keeping up with her. They ate from the buffet table laid out by volunteers and drank plenty of Coca Cola.

"I need some air," he told her as another song ended. He took her hand and led her outside to one of the benches.

"I've been to a few of these dances with Ann, but it is so much more fun with you here."

"Want a drink of this," he offered her the bottle of soda and slipped his arm behind her on the back of the bench. He was staring at her as she drank.

"What?"

"You are the most beautiful girl I think I have ever met."

"You think?"

"You are," he laughed. Richard leaned in and kissed her softly and gently. He watched her eyes open as he moved back, they smiled back at his along with those exquisite lips.

Richard saw Betsy several more times over the following weeks and continued to grow closer. They made several trips to Balboa Park, and a trip to Mission Beach as she promised.

Other than the color of the water, he would have guessed that he was at home. He could picture her there with him.

"I don't know what is going to happen to me, but I would like it if you would write to me." He looked down at her head laying on his arm and they laid together on a blanket on the sand. The moment was precious, flirting on intimate.

Betsy wrapped her arms around his neck and pulled him in until his lips met hers.

The sound of the waves crashing in, he did not hear her whisper, "I love you."

. . . .

On an early September morning all officers were called to the CO's office. Being among the lowest ranking officers, Richard quickly grabbed his jacket and checked his tie. He and the other officers were escorted to the office and received the news.

"We are calling all the men in; all leaves have been cancelled. Assemble your troops, we are shipping out at 1500 hours, destination Guadalcanal. Collect your gear and let's get moving. All immediate family will be notified of your new address, no one is to congest the phones. We have our orders men, dismissed."

Richard was able to get a note out to Betsy and asked her to write to him. "I hope to see you in the movies real soon. Don't give up your dream. Warmest regards, Richard." He also jotted a quick note and sent it out to his parents before going back to his room to roll his clothes and pack everything into his haversack and backpack. The company was assembled and the same message that was given to Richard was relayed to the soldiers.

Within hours, the lines of platoons marching in formation headed toward the docks. Richard caught a glimpse of Betsy who stood by the railing of the steps leading to her office. Richard acknowledged her frantic wave with a discreet nod and a quick flip of his hand.

She had seen the ship pull in that morning which typically meant it would be loaded up and set sail again. She was used to the troops parading on the dock, up the gangway off to places she couldn't conceive. Everyone's lives had changed so much over the past nine months. The world was in turmoil, she shook her head in disbelief as she watched her friend disappear around the corner. Betsy wondered if she would ever see Richard again. Theirs was not a romantic relationship; they had become close friends in a very short time. She could share anything with him. Betsy had told him one afternoon relaxing on the beach that she was afraid of going to Hollywood more than she was excited. She did not feel she could handle the rejection she foresaw. Richard was nothing but supportive and caring toward her. He shared his inside fear of combat. He knew and understood his duty. He was willing to give his life for his country if need be. Richard also had a responsibility to his men and make sure they made it back home. This was a priority in the back of his mind reminding him every time he looked at one of the soldiers.

After the forces boarded the converted freighter, each company was given an assignment on the ship. The sailors had their specific duties to be supplemented by the soldiers going to join the 164th Battalion as part of the first Army troops to land on Guadalcanal.

The officers settled in their quarters below deck while the soldiers spent the majority of their time on deck. They also slept on the deck while the freighter powered on through the Pacific Ocean toward their destination. During the 28 day trip the men would wake up and move before they were soaked from the sailors washing down the deck. They would line up for chow, eat their breakfast anywhere they could find a place to sit down. Afterward, they would get in line again to wash their mess gear. During the day the men practiced abandon ship drills while others studied the maps of the forbidding terrain of mountains and dormant volcanoes up to eight thousand feet high. There were steep ravines and deep streams and unforgiving jungles to memorize.

Richard walked along the deck with Matthew as the sun dipped in the October sky. He smoked his last cigarette before the smoking lamp went out and was careful not throw the butt overboard during the day or night. They were warned that even the smallest hint could warn the enemy of the reinforcements heading south. Each of them led their respective platoons through drills. He found Sgt. Harvey a bit lazy and unwilling to lead his squad. Richard hoped that his concerns would be put to rest before they landed. He did not want to have to report to the captain his fear for the men serviced under Harvey. He confided in Matthew who offered a few suggestions.

Word began to spread on the ship as they grew closer and closer to their destination. News of heavy fighting around the Savo Islands and Guadalcanal's southern tip spurred a lot of conversation, the anxiety was building. The Battle of Cape Esperance cleared the way for the arrival of the reinforcements. Their first stop, New Caledonia was a chance to get off the rolling ship. They had sailed past the Cook Islands and arrived from the south disembarking on the piers built by the Seabees. They had 24 hours before leaving on the transports protected by a task force of four cruisers and five destroyers. There would be no leaves granted, instead they were ordered to help unload the ship and load their supplies onto the ship they were transferring onto. Once they were done the soldiers horsed around in the water along the beach and ate and relaxed in the inviting sun thinking of what faced them over the horizon. The next morning the men gathered in the belly of the Landing Ship Tank (LST) on the tank deck and prepared to disembark.

Several men were sick from bobbing around on the water in the smaller craft across the channels. The smell of vomit was strong in the hull of the ship.

Richard looked over at Matthew who was readying his men for the short trip to the shore. The bow ramp dropped as the ship slid into the beach just as Richard had done so many times with his little sailboat on Martha's Vineyard. The landing was smooth, so much so that most of the men did not realize that they had arrived on Guadalcanal. The ship dropped its anchor out far enough to pull the ship back off the shore after its cargo was unloaded.

Richard's team was near the back of the deck and watched as the first platoons ushered onto the ramp into the knee-deep water to the sandy beach. Supplies were offloaded to be moved to their camp at Henderson Field when Japanese bombers flew overhead unloading their bombs on the arriving men. They ran for cover anywhere they could find.

Richard waved his men to where the Marines headed who were much more familiar with the island and the constant barrage of enemy fire than the soldiers were. The shelling continued for nearly two hours into the night. They watched trees splinter and the ground in front of them disappear. Richard cradled his Gerand M-1 rifle wishing there was something he could return fire at, but the 14-inch shells flew in from the Japanese battleships off the point. It was a sore introduction to the South Pacific. Richard was now living the numerous Newsreels he had seen lately at the theater with Betsy. He was thinking of her, wondering what she was doing and how much he would rather be dancing as much as he did not like to. They had so little time together, but the time they did spend was comforting and reassuring, he wanted to make it back to her.

By morning, Richard found his two sergeants and accounted for all of his men. Other squads were not as lucky as they gathered the dead and wounded. The soldiers found their gear and Richard had the men move the equipment into the camp and grabbed some chow. It had been a long, stressful night, but they had work to do.

Richard stooped to dodge the awning built from weaved palm leaves as he walked in for a briefing. The officers met in the green canvas tent with the Commanding Officer bringing them all up to date on the offensive. The new unit was to take the southeast position to the right of the more experienced Marine division. Each soldier gathered their supplies, filling their backpacks with ammunition, map case, and lifebelt. They each had a combat pack with a poncho to shield them from the rain that seemed to fall as often as the Japanese shells. Richard checked for socks, and several days of rations and as many packs of cigarettes as he could fit.

They started their trek through the jungle that was thick with trees and brush. The terrain was not like the forests they hiked through in

Virginia. After a couple of hours, they found a clearing where they could sit down, rest and eat their field rations. They did not know how long they would be out there, so it was important to save their supplies.

Three days after the squads left camp near Henderson Field, trudging through deep muddy ravines, streams and dense jungles, they arrived at their destination and found cover for the night. Guards were placed to watch for the Japanese who Richard knew from the reports that they were advancing from the south. Reinforcements of Japanese troops had been dropped by the Tokyo Express. Richard could feel them out there in the jungle.

He wasn't sure what time it was and if he had been asleep or not, but he stood straight up on his feet when he heard the screams, "Bonsai." The Japanese soldiers came running through the trees straight for him, the grass hissed as they ran through it. White flashes of light like fireflies fluttered across the field with the sound of gun fire. The men fought ferociously, firing their rifles, throwing grenades and hunting down the single Japanese who penetrated their line. They called in reinforcement in the form of anti-tank guns, mortar fire. Walls of fire exploded a hundred yards from their position as bullets flew through the air. Richard ordered his men to return fire and hold their position. His eyes adjusted to the black night, he squinted to see into the trees that easily could mimic the silhouette of Japanese solider. He threw another grenade while others did the same setting off a line of explosions eradicating the advancing troops. The Japanese backed off after the tremendous losses they incurred.

The next night brought almost an identical scene of events. Richard could hear their own aircraft defending the airstrip which was so valuable to the positioning of American forces in the Pacific. They dug in and fought off the enemy advances successfully. The few wounded were carried back to camp while patrols were sent into the jungle to eliminate the Japanese soldiers cut off from their division. They were starving in the jungles, but determined to defeat the American troops.

Each day for weeks Richard led his men back into the field. There were very few breaks or time to relax. When they did get some r&r, the soldiers went to the beach away from the crowded airstrip, played cards, read, or caught up on their mail. What he wouldn't give for a cold beer. The time off was short lived as they headed back out into the jungle. They walked past the line of Howitzers firing on the enemy lines. The artillery was a tactical factor in the battalion's nightly barrage on the Japanese. The squad came across a Japanese sniper, whose bullet screamed right by their heads. Harvey quickly took him out as the enemy soldier hidden in the leaves fell from the camouflaged hideout up in a tree. The Jap soldiers tied branches to their backs and arms and covered their helmets with leaves, it was a difficult target to see.

The patrol hurried over to where the enemy sniper fell while watching for other snipers. Harvey had made a clean shot through the neck. He had stepped up while battling through the forests. Richard was proud of the sergeant and even recommended him for a silver star. Harvey had defended their position during their first engagement with the enemy, rolling from gun to gun firing at the Japanese forces. He was turning into a heroic model for the men.

They heard the expression that 'death was only five feet away', which rang true in so many of the battles they endured. Richard and his team of ten other men sat on a barren hill hidden in the tall grass. Rain wasn't the issue this afternoon as the sun beat down on them. Sweating in the sun and itching from the mosquitoes was not uncommon. The island was relentless and beginning to wear on them. He savored the moment with the breeze blowing through the swaying grass. Richard could only imagine how the Marines felt having been there for several grueling months. He looked out on the bay; they had a great panoramic view from their vantage point.

There were at least thirty ships sitting in the harbor of deep blue and green water. He watched the small caps break on the surface when an ominous dark wave descended on the vessels. Richard pulled out his binoculars to see an air raid had come in to a furry of black anti-aircraft fire exploding from the ships. Black puffs of smoke replaced the puffy white clouds and the Japanese planes began to fall from the sky. Richard waved off one of his men who jumped to his feet and started to yell for the American pilots intercepting and chasing down the planes trying to escape.

"Get down will ya!" He demanded. "You'll get your fool head shot off." He had no intention on a grunt soldier giving away their position to another sniper and told him so in a verbal thrashing. He had never had to speak to anyone in such a manner and did not enjoy doing so.

They watched the chase move farther out on the horizon. The last enemy plane made a streak of fire and smoke across the sky before it splashed into the ocean. Richard could not see a parachute like he did with some of the other planes that went down. The Sun shined in brilliant bands through the smoke on the American fleet as if to salute their triumph.

Richard rose to his feet, "let's move out." He held his gun firmly, ready to shoot if needed.

They continued their patrol around the ridge with no resistance. That night they returned to camp and immediately set to helping dig new bunkers which were used to store supplies and to protect the soldiers. They used their shovels to unearth the deep holes and covered them with logs and sandbags.

"Sir, this will never protect us from a direct hit from the Japanese."

"No, but it will protect you from flying shrapnel. Button it up and let's get it done." Richard almost laughed at the structure, thinking it would never protect them.

Richard rested in his tent and shivered uncontrollably. He wasn't cold, rather soaked in sweat and filthy from the mud on the island. The rain pelted down on them daily, for now he was protected from the soaking forest rain. The weekly chore of patching the tents protected them from the rain and insects. Richard assumed the shaking was his nerves; although, he did not want his men to see how shaken he was from the constant attacks. It was more than anyone could ever imagine.

His body ached all over and his hands were blistered from the hot barrel of his gun. Richard closed his eyes while thinking of Betsy who was most likely working through the piles of paperwork at the shipyard. He was woken up by Matthew who opened the tent flap and tossed a string bound pack at him.

"Merry Christmas, mail call buddy." Matthew settled in beside Richard and sat back with his letters. "I got a letter from my dad. He received the government contract from the Quartermaster. He will be supplying the kitchens for our FIELD RATIONS's. Isn't that a hoot? Can you imagine some real food? No more <u>Spam</u> and Vienna Sausages."

"Merry Christmas? Wow, I can't believe it has been over a year since Pearl Harbor." Richard sat up and looked through the envelopes Matthew brought him. "I got a letter from Betsy, two from my mom and one from Charlie's parents."

"What is Betsy up to?" Matthew looked up from his mail to hear about Richard's news.

"She is still working at the shipyard. She and Ann went to the beach with a couple of sailors. There was a dance at the YMCA and there was a film crew there filming for the newsreels. She said she was talking to the camera man and told him about wanting to go to Hollywood." He folded the letter and put it back into the envelope. He hoped all of her dreams would come true. He would like to see her again someday and figured that would be highly unlikely. They had lives very different from one another, hers on the west coast with the line of soldiers and his on the east if he made it back home.

"She is a sweet girl. Anderson had some stories about her roommate, I don't think her mother would want to hear. She can't handle the giggle water."

"Good thing Betsy is nothing like Ann," Richard defended.

"Nothing like her?" Matthew never wanted to pry regarding the relationship between Richard and Betsy. He assumed it was romantic. Richard assured Matthew that they were friends and nothing more.

"She is a respectable girl, Benton." He spoke. Richard got off his cot and found a piece of writing paper in his footlocker. Matthew backed off and settled down to his own letter as Richard wrote to Betsy.

Betsy,

How I miss the realization of being on the same continent with my family and friends for Christmas. Guadalcanal is heaven and hell rolled into one. The Pacific islands are incredible, there are times when I sit and look out to sea gazing at the other islands, I find it hard to believe that we are at war. I have seen some ugly things as well as some very beautiful sights. Looking at the hills, there are patches of light green valleys and grass and patches of deep green jungles.

The sunrise is a spectacular glow peeking through the low strips of cotton like clouds. The sunsets are equally magnificent, burning orange on the horizon. The vultures are big enough to carry you away and the bats take over the camp at night looking for fruit fallen from the trees. The white cockatoos are handsome and sit in the trees and laugh at us when we are working. There are a few that are brave enough to fly down and take a piece of papaya from our hands. Another large black bird with a white head fills the trees and causes quite a commotion when they all start calling out. I have seen plenty of lizards, long ugly things that run around our feet at night. It was very unsettling at first, but I have grown used to them now.

If you don't like insects, this is not the place for you. There are spiders of every size and dragonflies of every imaginable color where ever you look. The worst are the ants. If you stand still for too long or drop a piece of food they attack immediately. The jungles are thick with plants that I have never seen before and likely never see again.

I think you are swell for writing to me. The mail does not come often enough, today brought me a sweet surprise reading your letter. Matthew brought my letters while I was catching a nap. He sends his regards. We are both well although we could use a good meal, a beer and some good music..."

"Colonel wants to see us." Gibson stuck his head into the bunker. "We need to hightail it over to his office, sounds like he has some dope for us."

Richard tucked the letter in a book so he could finish it later. The three men hurried over as instructed to join the other officers who were already there.

"We are sending part of the Marine units to Australia and your squads be picking up more of the patrol details." The Colonel announced. "The Marines are exhausted and there are several were suffering from Malaria. Anderson, you take your men for burial detail."

They would bury the fallen soldiers in a hole, cover it with lime and bulldoze over them. It seemed an insensitive burial, but they had to dispose of the bodies to avoid even more sickness than what was already looming over them. Gibson took his men over to gather what ammunition they could find and resupply each of the units. Sherrott went to the airfield to help with repairs. The daily raids pounded the airstrip with holes which impaired the timely launch of American planes. The PBY Catalina's where painted black and nicknamed the "Black Cats." They flew mainly at night taking out enemy targets. The pilot's stories amused the soldiers while they joked about taking the shrapnel and other junk from the Japanese bombings of the airfield and dumped it back on the targets. It seemed like an insane ploy, but they did it to harass and irritate the enemy.

Richard and Matthew were assigned to have their men remove and salvage what they could from the communication building that had been blown up by a Japanese shell. There were sun-soaked boards lying all over the ground where the building once stood. Most pieces were too small and would be used for kindling. The larger pieces would be used to rebuild a suitable structure for the radios that kept the division in contact with the ships and nearby islands.

Someone had taken empty Field Ration cans and erected a makeshift Christmas tree and decorated it with flowers from the area. It was a nice contradiction to the war they were fighting. The soldiers were piling the last of the wood that they felt could be used again when they heard the rumble of aircraft. Habit turned their gaze skyward to see their planes coming in after an all-night raid.

"Didn't our guys come back about an hour ago?" Richard seemed to remember the pilots walking up to camp to get some chow while singing Christmas carols. They were more worried about their bellies than the casualties.

He looked up again, "take cover." He yelled. The planes were enemy fighters and not their own after all. He looked over at Matthew; whose eyes were wide and full of concern.

"Get out of here." Matthew started running for the nearest bunker.

The plane whined through the sky, the sound grew louder and louder until there was a terrible explosion. Richard felt his leg burn and he was pushed to the ground. Men were running everywhere; he could see the bunker but couldn't get himself up to reach it. Something was holding him down. He heard men screaming.

The wing of the plane somersaulted through the camp. He watched it slide across the ground, kicking up dirt as it came to a stop. Everything was happening so fast, yet it seemed like they were moving in slow motion. It was so damn loud.

The explosions continued while the bombs from the Japanese fighter crashed to the ground with the rest of the plane. The noise was more than he could handle, the bombs were too close. Richard could feel the heat from the nearby fire on his face while smoke filled his lungs. Shrapnel was flying in every direction and trees were reduced to toothpicks. Smoke billowed from the decimated camp. He could barely see as he attempted once more to drag himself toward the safety of the bunker, clawing at the dirt until everything went dark.

Richard woke up lying on the ground on a stretcher. He could still smell smoke, and then realized it was his clothes. Trying to sit up was useless, he couldn't move. He raised his head enough to look down at his legs and noticed that his pants were burnt and bloody. He was in excruciating pain. A medic was kneeling beside the body beside him bandaging the other victim's head. Richard couldn't tell who it was; the face was covered with gauze. The medic noticed Richard was awake.

"Just stay still, there is a transport on its way to get you guys out of here."

"How many?" He asked. "How many wounded?"

"Thirty-one last count. You guys got hit hard. The air raid sirens never even went off." There was no Condition Red called to the men. The medic checked Richard's bleeding and gave him some Morphine from a small brown packet. "We are going to move you guys to the Field Hospital. You hold on." He assured Richard that he would live and moved on to tend to more of the wounded. The planes threw them a good blow. Usually, they have some type of warning. Today they did not.

Richard drifted off to sleep again. He dreamt he was walking through the deep jungle eating a piece of fruit playing with the birds that flew down from the trees to him. It was a rare occasion that it was not raining and he wasn't knee deep in mud. His boots had been set aside so he could walk across the meadow in his bare feet. He was enjoying the sunshine and the cool breeze moving across the valley. Clouds were gliding across the sky like the Navy ships sailing through the "Slot." The dream turned into his worst nightmare when the bird sitting on his shoulder turned into a Jap soldier biting his ear and clawing at his face. Richard tried feverishly to knock the bird down to the ground and get it off of him. More of the birds flew down attacking him as he swat at them flying around his head. Feathers blocked his view of the valley and the bay; he fought to see what was happening around him. He grew tired and felt like giving in to the enemy then thought better of it. All of the birds turned into the enemy with one relentless strike after another. He continued his struggle fending off the attack. They wouldn't give up; harassing him with their awful screams that turned into screams too familiar "Bonsai." He could feel the pain mounting in his body when the captain entered the dream, 'stand down soldier, stand down.'

The medics were holding Richard's arms trying to keep him from hurting himself. "Hold him down," he said.

Richard was thrashing around on the stretcher. He had already been moved to the field hospital near the shore where the Doctor had looked at his injuries. He had survived the attack, but he was not in good shape. He would need surgery to repair the damage to his leg. They gave him some of the new drug they had to help with any infection. He was given a dose of penicillin along with more morphine. Finally, the pain subsided enough for Richard to rest again. He fought off sleeping fearing the awful nightmares would return. Richard couldn't help but to succumb to the pain killer.

The field hospital was a simple tent erected with wooden poles covered with green canvas and screened walls. There was a large white square on the top with a red cross inside. Wounded were carried into the structure and placed on cots or left on the stretchers on the ground. The concrete slab was washed down several times daily to keep the dirt and dust to a minimum. There was a bottle of plasma hanging on a pole next to Richard's litter. The medical staff did what patching up they could do and tagged the wounded by priority for transport. The less severe wounds would be treated and the men sent back to their units for action. Those who were deemed to not be able to return to combat were loaded onto the transports headed to New Caledonia and then transferred to a hospital ship.

CHAPTER 4 Long Beach

· · · ·

Richard was oblivious to his new surroundings. He was in and out of consciousness throughout the trip north before he and the other injured soldiers were placed on the white hospital ship. Marked on the side with a large red cross, they were supposed to have safe passage through the shipping lanes carrying the wounded back to the United States. He was scheduled for surgery the day after their passage began to attempt to repair the damage to his leg. The wing and the engine of the Japanese fighter had skid through the camp cutting Richard's leg clear through to the bone just above the knee. He would walk again, but traversing the hills and terrain of the island would be too much on the injury. Doctors warned him that following the procedure he would most likely have a limp for the remainder of his life.

Richard lay in his bunk most of the time recuperating. The bunks were made of metal frames with woven canvas strips forming a hammock for the patients. He was thankful for the bottom bunk. The wound was cleaned and the dressings were changed daily. To prevent infection, he was given penicillin a fairly new drug that had proved successful in Europe.

It was two weeks before he dragged himself out of bed with the help of an orderly into the wheelchair by his bed. He wanted to get up on deck, but the stairways restricted him getting up top. Richard sat in the recreation room for a little while and talked to a few of the other soldiers. The large bandages made sitting too long uncomfortable, but he enjoyed the distraction more than lying in bed staring at the white metal ceiling above. Most of the soldiers had similar stories to share about the battles they had endured in the Soloman Islands, Tulagi, and the Gilbert Islands.

Each day he sat in the recreation room longer than the other. He learned to play cribbage, but most of the time they played cards.

A private was reading a letter he wrote to his dog. "Dear old pal. You know, I've been wondering." Several of the men laughed. "When a guys out here, a long way from home, he does a lot of thinking and a lot of wondering. I've been wondering if mom ever reads you any of my letters."

"Most guys are writing to their girl and this guy is writing to his dog," someone else yelled out.

The letter caused Richard to remember the letter he had been writing to Betsy before he was wounded, he wondered where the rest of his belongings would wind up. Richard had inquired several times about Matthew and the men in his unit. Information was sparse but he was able to find out that Matthew has sustained burns to his face and was not responsive to the urging of the doctors. Richard was the only member of his unit to receive injuries bad enough to evacuate him. The others remained on Guadalcanal to continue fighting the Japanese without him.

Finally, the ship arrived in Long Beach, California slipping in to whistles from other ships and waves from those standing on the docks. Some of the wounded were loaded onto the litters and carried off the ship while others were wheeled down in wheelchairs or hobbled down with crutches to the waiting transports. The U.S. coast was a welcome site as he was carried across the deck along the rails to the ramp leading to U.S. soil. There was a lot of activity on the pier unloading the ship to make room for another. The ambulances were loaded and sent on their way as another pulled up waiting for more wounded. Richard and the others were taken to an Army hospital for further evaluation and rehabilitation.

• • • •

Richard quickly started therapy to get him up on his feet. He was given crutches to help him get around without having to use the wheelchair. The doctors were pleased with how Richard's leg was healing. He needed to work on getting the muscles strong enough to hold his weight again so he was taken to the gym every day. He considered himself lucky when he looked around and saw that the majority of the soldiers there were missing limbs. Men moved around on crutches with one leg of their pajama bottoms hanging limp or tucked into the waist line. He read a lot during the day and they watched movies at night to pass the time until the lucky ones were released to go home or reassigned for another duty. Richard figured that most of these men would be sent home. Once a week he would attend adjustment classes preparing the soldiers to face civilian life again and deal with the horrors that they had witnessed first-hand.

After therapy, Richard made his way to the recreation room where there was a piano. It had been too long since being able to sit in front of the keyboard and relax. There were a few soldiers in the room who didn't seem to mind Richard's playing. He watched the other men while he played some of his favorite tunes thinking of the men he left behind in the Pacific. Richard watched a particular soldier sitting in a wheelchair by the window gazing out at the sparkling ocean. The plain white walls did not lend much to the healing process and most of the men ached for some semblance of the outside world. The soldier's head was covered in bandages and Richard could see some of the scars on the exposed skin. There was something familiar. Richard stopped playing and continued to study the man sitting alone in the same hospital pajamas the rest of them wore and a blanket covering his legs.

Richard crossed the room to where the man sat and asked if he could join him at the table next to the window.

"Makes you want to get out there and feel the sunshine." He looked at the man who gave no response, he sat looking out the window.

The man finally met Richard's stare. He was tired of how people looked at him and sometimes wondered why he had not just died on the island he was stationed at. He had no life anymore and most likely never would. All of his dreams were over with no hope of leading a normal life ever again. His heart ached worse than the wounds he suffered in the war.

"Matthew? Matthew, is that you?" Richard could feel the excitement run through his body when he recognized the eyes of the bandaged figure.

Again, there was no response from the man that Richard could see. His eyes blinked, Richard could see the pain in the steel grey eyes that looked back at him. Richard could see that he had been burned on his hands that held the arms of the wheelchair. He assumed the bandages on his head were covering burns on his face as well. Only his eyes and lips were visible. The lips pursed slightly as if trying to say something and the soldier's eyes welled up as he recognized his friend. "It is you, isn't it?"

"Rishir..." He managed to get the slurred words out.

"I can't believe it is you. I couldn't find out anything, no one would tell me how you were."

Matthew only shook his head, but Richard didn't understand.

"What did the doctors say?" Richard could see that Matthew was struggling. He was so happy to see him and did not want to push Matthew into talking. Richard figured the fire and the burns injured his voice in some way. Matthew continued to look at Richard. He looked down at his scarred hands and then at Richard's legs with questions in his eyes. Richard started to describe his injury when a nurse came to take Matthew back to his ward.

"He cannot hear you." She spoke.

"What, the bandages over his ears?"

"That is just part of it. But he cannot hear you."

Richard looked at Matthew, he was so sorry for him. Richard had been around plenty of deaf people on Martha's Vineyard. His family had a history of deafness and his relative George Tilton had sailed on the same ship as Laurent Clerc and Thomas Gallaudet as they began developing American Sign Language he knew the story well. Richard was no stranger to the culture that Matthew was now a part of. He patted Matthew's shoulder; he didn't know the extent of the burns and was very careful not to hurt him. Richard hoped Matthew could at least read his lips as he told his friend he would see him later before the nurse wheeled Matthew away.

Their time at the hospital went by slowly. There was little to do to keep him occupied. Richard sat with Matthew each day in silence. He shared his letters from home and helped Matthew when he tried to write to his parents. He asked one of the nurses if she could find something about sign language so he could start helping Matthew learn to communicate. She told him that Matthew would go through classes when he was transferred back to the East Coast, but she would see what she could find for them in the meantime.

Richard was sitting in the commons writing a letter to his parents. He knew they had received word of his injury from the State Department and had sent word as soon as he could that he was stateside and doing 'fine'. He did not want his mother to worry; he was in one piece and better off than the majority making a premature return. Her letter was full of motherly concern and joy that her son survived the war. His parents were eager to see him and wished him well.

"Hey soldier." Betsy slid her hands on Richard's shoulders when she walked up behind him.

"Oh my gosh." He said. Richard couldn't believe she was standing beside him. He had thought of her so much and here she was.

"It is so good to see you. I hadn't heard anything from you in so long, I was afraid..." There were a few whistles when Betsy pulled up a chair and took Richard's hands in hers. Betsy had a new permanent wave in her hair and was wearing lip rouge.

"How did you find me?" He was so glad to see his friend even while sitting there in the pajama pants and hospital gown that he was wearing.

"Ann checks the list of men coming in on the ships every day for the guys she has met." Betsy was being nice when referring to Ann's acquaintances. They both knew Ann had not been discreet when it came to her dates with the soldiers when they came to San Diego. "She saw your name and called me."

"She called you? Are you still working at the shipyard?"

"No, but let me know how you are really doing first." She looked him up and down. He seemed to have come back intact.

"Took a wing of a Jap fighter to my leg. Almost took it clean off," he laughed.

"You are very lucky." Betsy looked around the room at the soldiers and the various wounds from missing arms and legs, to scars deeper than she knew.

"It was really bad there. We were up all night trying to hold off the attacks and then working most of the day. There were times when we would be up three days straight with no sleep." He could see the tears welling up in Betsy's eyes. He stopped describing the horrific conditions so he would not upset her. "So, tell me, why were you not working?"

"Now don't get too excited, it really isn't much yet but I hope to get into some big pictures soon." She wiggled in her chair with excitement, her dreams were beginning to come true. "We, Ann and I were at a USO dance and there was this guy there filming a newsreel and pulling Marines for extras in a movie. I was singing that night. I started singing at the dances, kind of my contribution to the boys. Anyway, this suit comes up and hands me his number and tells me to call. He said he can probably use me in a picture. Isn't that a scream?" She was talking so fast Richard found it hard to keep up with her.

"That is fantastic, Betsy." He said.

"I thought he was giving me a line. Turns out he's the Darb."

Richard listened intently. It was nice to have her there and to have something to do. In the days he had been in Long Beach, Richard's agenda consisted of exams, physical therapy, reading and an occasional card game. He was eager to get home to his folks.

"I moved last month," Betsy continued. "I called Mr. Jefferson and told him I was in town and he asked me to come down to the studio for a screen test."

"That's just swell Betsy." He said. Richard was getting tired and his leg was beginning to ache, but he did not want Betsy to leave. "What was that like?"

"I was so nervous." She took off her grey wool coat that she was still wearing and hung it over the back of another one of the chairs at the table. "I sing. I have never tried to read lines. So, I did it and Mr. Jefferson said I did fine. I haven't heard anything yet."

"I am so happy for you." Richard put his hands on hers in a supportive gesture. Betsy looked at their hands and smiled at Richard.

"I am glad to see you are alright."

"I am, and even better now that you're here." He said. Richard was surprised that she made the trip from LA to see him. She was the only friend he had here. "Want to go for a walk. I think the guys are starring at you."

"Who?" Betsy asked while she turned to look around the room to see what Richard was talking about.

Richard reached for the crutches sitting on the floor beside his chair. "Everyone is going to be asking me later who the Sheba was with me today." He laughed at her reaction.

"You're sweet." Betsy said with a giggle. She helped him with his crutches and he stood as straight as he could next to her.

"There is a garden area in the center of the hospital. All of the wards have access to it."

Betsy followed Richard and held the door for him while they walked into the courtyard. There were a few other patients sitting on the benches or in wheelchairs. He picked out one of the white benches and waited for Betsy to sit down and then sat down beside her.

"Tell me about your friends, are they still in the South Pacific?" She remembered some of the guys Richard hung out with but she couldn't remember their names.

"They are all there, except for Matthew." Richard looked down at his own leg and tried to remember how lucky he was. "He was hurt pretty bad. His face and hands were burned when the Jap plane came down on us. He can't hear either."

"Temporarily, or for good?"

"For good from what his nurse told me. The explosion ruptured his eardrums. The burns will heal but I'm afraid that he won't get his hearing back." Richard had not thought much about the day they were wounded, he told Betsy as much as he thought she could handle. "We were working a detail, cleaning up what was left of the radio building. It was where we received all of our communication. It had been blown to kindling the week before in a bombing. Other guys were raking the dirt back into the holes that the bombs made in the ground. We heard the planes and then I remember the high pitch whine of a bomb dropping, then the sound of the plane got really close – too close. The Jap pilot came screaming through the trees right where we were working. I remember seeing the big red sun on the wing coming right at me. I don't remember much after that. I'm really worried about Matthew. They said he was trapped under the plane while it was on fire."

"He'll be fine Richard. Before you know it, you two will be dancing with all the girls again." Betsy had some bigger questions for him, she wasn't sure when to ask him. She wanted to see how he felt before making any assumptions regarding their relationship. "What are you going to do when you get out of here?"

"I want to go home and see my parents. My mom must be worried to death."

Betsy shook her head agreeing with him that he should see his parents. "I hope you will write to me when you go home."

"You will be so busy with your movies that you will never write me back."

"Of course I will. I may never even get to be in a film." She hated the prospect that most girls never get a starring role and spend their lives in the chorus or as an extra.

They sat in the courtyard and talked for hours when an orderly found him. It was time for his physical therapy before dinner. Betsy walked back into the building with them and left Richard with a hug and a kiss on the cheek. She was glad he was alive; he didn't know how glad she was. She whispered, "I love you" as he limped away.

Richard received word that he would be shipped home the following week with several other men. Most were being transferred to John Hopkins's Hospital while others like Richard would actually get to return to their homes. He let his parents know by telegram and eventually received a reply that his room would be ready for him and that they couldn't wait for his return. Richard also called Betsy and let her know the good news.

Betsy fought to hide her disappointment that Richard would be leaving California. "I am happy for you. I know how badly you want to get home to see your parents." Her screen test gained her positive reviews and an offer to sing background in a movie about two Vaudeville performers. Betsy's role would be very small, but it was a start. "I will write to you every week."

"You had better. I want to hear about everything you are doing." Richard was happy for his friend, but ready to get on with his life. He appreciated her friendship. "I'll come back and go see one of your films with you."

"Now you are getting way ahead of yourself. I just got my first small part."

"And it is just the beginning." He said. Richard smiled at Betsy, she was a good friend to him and had been extremely sweet when she came to Long Beach to see him during his recovery.

• • • •

Richard could see the island coming into view as they sailed closer and closer on the small boat. He could make out the Gay Head Lighthouse and the clay seaside cliffs. There were a few sail boats on the water under the blue streaked sky. Richard lifted his head to take in the familiar brisk, salt air, his father sensed his son's emotions and patted his shoulder.

"Your mother wants to have a big welcome home party as soon as you are settled in."

"I hope she gives me some time."

"Everyone is anxious to see you son. They are just glad you are coming home." Timothy left out the fact that so many young men from the island would never return.

They walked off of the steamer that carried them over to the island. Richard used his crutches to support himself with his father holding onto his arm. The car was parked on the side of the road waiting their arrival. Timothy loved his 1935 Chevrolet Master Deluxe. It was a unique blue when most where black and had gauges with cream faces with brown numbers rather than the previous year's black face with white numbers. Richard had spent many weekends polishing his father's car for him.

"Car looks good dad." Richard's own Chevrolet Sport Roadster was parked at the house waiting for him. Richard had saved his money, sending it home for his mother to keep in a bank account as well as the war bond he had. He hoped that after finding a job he could get one of the newer models with turn signals and other new inventions.

"Oh, Richard it is so good to have you home." Annette Moeller opened the door as soon as she saw her husband and son walk up the steps. She had been waiting anxiously for her son's return from the war.

"It's great to be home mom." Richard hobbled on his crutches into the familiar house. Not much had changed since he left for the Pacific or even college. He was a different person now than from when he was younger, running through the house out the back screen door letting it slam shut behind him. Richard loved growing up in Martha's Vineyard with the water and the people from various parts of the country.

"What are they saying about your service? They didn't discharge you." Timothy Moeller steadied the chair for Richard to sit down as the three adults sat in the kitchen at the simple enamel table.

"Will you have to go back?" Annette assumed that Richard was home for good, but no one had really said anything before now. She put the tea kettle on the Wedgewood stove and joined them at the table.

"I will eventually. I have some leave time to get back in shape. I am just waiting on my new orders. It was crazy over there." His father shot him a glance reminding Richard not to discuss some of the details in front of his mother.

"You just take it easy here while you can. I have your room all fixed up for you." Annette found it hard to sit still and was up again tending to the tea and digging in the ice box. "I have some chicken in the oven for dinner. I'm sorry, it isn't much but we are rationing."

"Anything is great mom. I lived on field rations for months and a home cooked meal sounds wonderful."

"Your mother updated the family album with clippings from the paper about your service." Timothy showed him the news articles that Annette had pasted in the leather book which dated back before the turn of the century and his ancestors. Richard had paged through the book so many times reading about his Great-great grandfather and is voyage on the Mary Augusta, his Great grandfather's service in the army, and even his father's service in Great War.

Richard spent the next two weeks recovering from his injuries when a telegram was delivered with his new orders. He was to report to the Quartermaster Headquarters in New York to work in the finance department.

"I can drive you up if you would like." Timothy was up in Richard's room with him while he packed the few things he needed to take with him.

"I was going to take my car so I have it there. I can handle the clutch pretty well now." Richard looked around the room that he had grown up in and was leaving yet again. He didn't know when he would be back. It had been three months since he was injured at Guadalcanal and he was getting around with a cane rather than the crutches. He still had a visible limp and pain that he would most likely always have to deal with.

"I packed some sandwiches for your trip." Annette handed Richard a brown sack. She had tears in her eyes as she watched her son assemble his bags by the door.

"I will be back mom. Think of Charlie and some of the other guys that never made it back. I am one of the lucky ones." He looked around the room that he knew so well. The couch he sat on nervously with his first date, the chair that his father sat in with his newspaper and pipe, and the fireplace that he hauled endless stacks of wood in for.

"You had better get going if you want to catch the ferry."

• • • •

Richard's office consisted of a room with ten desks in a building taken over by the government for military use. He was given a desk in the middle of the drab room. There was a stack of papers on the desk waiting to be reviewed and filed. He was in charge of coding requisitions to the correct department. He was given a quick briefing of his responsibilities and sat down to get to work. He noticed the CO come out of his office a few times and drop off more paperwork to one of the desks. Overall, it was a quiet first morning, nothing like the chaos he had experienced.

"Welcome to the unit Moeller." The CO came over to Richard.

"Thank you, sir."

"Served in the Pacific I understand."

"Yes, sir."

"We appreciate what you did son. If there is anything you need you just let someone know. Any of these flatfoots will give you a hand."

"Thank you, sir." With that the CO disappeared back into his office and shut the door.

"You some kind of hero?" Corporal Kent at the desk next to his questioned him. The CO rarely talks to anyone.

"No. Just caught an unlucky Jap wing to my leg and got sent stateside."

"I wouldn't call that unlucky, but I would have given anything to get my hands on one of those Japs. My brother bought it over in France. I signed up as soon as I got out of high school, but I got stuck here."

"I saw my fill, but I would have preferred staying there and helping my men."

"Well, it's still swell to have you here. You will have to tell me all about it sometime."

Richard had received a Purple Heart, an Asiatic Pacific Campaign Ribbon and two Bronze Stars. He did not consider himself a hero, but was thankful for what we were able to accomplish in his service overseas.

"A few of us are going to the diner to get some supper, do you want to come along?"

"Sure," Richard nodded and set aside the papers he was working on.

He ate across the street with John Kent, and a couple of the other guys in the office. He sat next to the window and watched the traffic on the street and the people walking down the sidewalk. It seemed like no one even realized what was going on around the world as they went about their daily business. Richard took another bite out of his sandwich as Kent told the others about Richard's service in Guadalcanal.

"How many did you kill?"

"I don't know, it was outrageous over there and you just didn't count." Richard thought that Kent was overly enthusiastic for someone who really had no understanding to what was really going on.

"Tell us about the Jap plane that got you." The other guys were listening intently while Richard recounted some of the story for them.

"It was Christmas morning; I don't even know what time it was. We were cleaning up from a previous bombing when I heard a plane coming in. It was not the same sound as when our planes came in, it was a higher pitch and coming in quickly. I remember seeing the plane coming straight at us. We were scrambling for the bunkers and I got hit as it cart wheeled across the ground. There was dirt flying and trees crashing down all around me."

"Wow. I got as far as boot camp and then I was assigned here." Decker was in his early twenties the best that Richard could guess. "I mean, you see all of the News Reels but I never got to talk to anyone who has seen some real action."

"You will get to talk to plenty once this war is over. Plenty of guys will have seen more action than I did.

"Our troops are giving the Germans hell right now in Tunisia." Kent kept everyone posted to the current events regarding the confrontations around the world.

The group finished their lunch and headed back to the office. It was a familiar scene seeing several military personnel in uniform on the street, just the same, the group caught several glances from the girls as they passed.

"Watch out for Decker, he's doll dizzy. Different girl every weekend." Kent shook his head. "I don't know how he does it. I have a better-looking mug than he does."

Richard enjoyed the banter between them. He was enjoying his first day and getting to know some of the people he would be working with. He set his Coke on his desk and picked up the requisitions he had been working on. He looked at the bottle and thought how great it would have been to have months ago instead of the stale water they drank. He thought about the guys back at the canal. They had most likely moved to another front by now after the Japanese withdrew from Guadalcanal in January. Richard caught as much information as he could in the office. So much was confidential, but it was more than he could get listening to the radio or watching the Newsreels.

He left that evening for the apartments that the officers stayed in. The building was a Brownstone converted into several living spaces; it was sufficient for his needs. He walked up the steps and through the front door and then up another flight of steps to the room he was assigned to. It beat the barracks and the tents or the occasional mud hole he had become accustomed to. There was a green couch in the center of the room, a wood table and two matching chairs in the kitchen area. He made a mental note to go to the hardware store to buy a radio for some sort of entertainment. He took off the green uniform jacket, loosened his tie and sat on the couch. The neighborhood was pretty quiet and a short walk to the office if the weather was nice enough. Spring was well at hand, so the walks would be pleasant.

Richard's daily routine did not change much, he went to work and then went to his apartment and listened to his new radio or watched out the window. The trees were all in full bloom and the birds chirped outside.

He looked at the mail that he brought up with him, a letter from Betsy! He tore open the envelope that still smelled like her. He could picture her auburn hair pulled back behind her ears reading the script she wrote about. Betsy finished the film she had been working on in January and was working on another. She had a supporting role. Her career was really starting to take off. Richard smiled; he was so happy for her. She also mentioned that she was coming to New York and wanted to take him to see the first film she appeared in although it was a brief appearance. She left her number and address for him and he decided to go ahead and try to call her.

The phone was downstairs and he had only used it a couple of times to talk to his folks. He dialed the number she sent while looking at his watch trying to figure out what time it would be in California.

"Betsy? It's Richard." He yelled into the phone. He had a terrible connection when he heard her pick up. "I got your letter and thought I would call you. When are you coming East?"

"It is great to hear your voice, Richard. It is raining here, so we did not have to go to the set today."

"I'm glad I caught you. So, when are you coming to New York?"

"How about next week? I will finish my scenes this week and then have two weeks before I have more scenes to shoot."

"Next week sounds great. Sounds exciting all this Hollywood stuff."

"I love it. I get tired, but I am having a great time. I saw Frank Sinatra at the studio the other day, it was killer diller."

"Really. Wow, I am so impressed."

"It wasn't much, he didn't even see me."

"He will, and so will all the other leading men."

"I have to go, but I will call you and let you know my plans, okay?"

"That is great Betsy, I can't wait to see you." Richard finished his call and went back up to his apartment. He skipped up the steps excited that Betsy would be coming to town.

• • • •

Friday after work, Richard threw a bag into his Roadster and drove down to Washington, DC. He had been following Matthew's progress and knew that he had been transferred closer to home. He was going through transitional training to help him to adjust to his new situation.

When Richard got to the hospital visiting hours were almost over, but he decided to go in for a short while anyway.

"Hi de ho pal." Richard said absently as he opened the door to Matthew's room and stepped in. He was sitting up in bed and turned toward the movement in the room.

Richard wasn't sure how to communicate with him so he waved his hand and smiled.

Matthew had a pen and a pad of paper on the table next to him and reached out for it. "What are you doing out here?" Matthew wrote.

Richard turned the pad toward him and jotted down his reply. "I came to see you."

"Not much into visitors, but thanks."

"Well, you're stuck with me. I came down to spend the weekend with you." He slid the pad back to him.

"Thanks." Matthew had changed a lot. He still wasn't sure how to deal with not being able to hear. His scars were healing, but he was scarred mentally which was more difficult to heal.

"Visiting hours are over." A nurse looked in and excused Richard while she checked on Matthew.

"I'll be back in the morning," Richard jotted on the notepad and left with a salute. He left the hospital and decided to drive around the city. He drove to the Capitol and parked so he could walk around. Richard was able to go up into the Washington Monument and look south toward the Lincoln Memorial which was lit up. He could see people moving around like ants beyond the Reflecting pool. There were more people crossing either of the two bridges across the pool and several lights still in the Naval buildings along the side of the grounds. Even in the moonlight, he could see the beginning Cherry Blossom blooms.

• • • •

Richard needed more information about the language that could help Matthew. First thing in the morning he jumped up and looked in the phone book for the closest library.

He walked into the one he found between his hotel and the hospital. He followed the signs to the area he thought he needed and walked up and down the aisles. Richard stopped and stared at the girl standing at the table just beyond the shelf of books he was walking by. He tried to look away, but he just couldn't get past the pull he felt. She looked up at him and smiled, then looked back down at the books she was picking up to put away.

"Do you know where the section on languages is?" He knew the section was right there, but he just had to talk to her. He thought maybe she was working there.

She didn't respond, but he just stood there, he couldn't move. When she turned toward him, her arms loaded with the books, she smiled again.

"I'm looking for a book."

The girl smiled, but shook her head. That's when Richard noticed her badge that stated she was a deaf volunteer. He gestured to his ear and moved his hands as if he were opening a book.

"Book," he mouthed. "Teach sign language."

She walked him over to the section he needed, nodded with a smile and walked away with her books.

Richard watched her walk away and then picked a book up that he thought he could use to help Matthew. Richard was not unaccustomed to the language. He remembered the stories of his relative, George Tilton who was with Thomas Gallaudet in the early 1800's when he was refining American Sign Language while crossing the Atlantic.

George's son, Richard's Great Grandfather was deaf and attended the University here in Washington DC.

He looked for the girl as he walked to the front of the library to check out his book. He couldn't see her, but her vision was imbedded in his mind. Richard tucked the book under his arm and headed to the hospital to spend some time with his friend. He had the whole weekend to show Matthew some signs before heading back to New York to see Betsy.

Richard worked with Matthew Saturday afternoon and then walked over to the Red Cross recreation center for a while. Other than not being able to hear any longer, Matthew was in good condition considering what they had been through. He had been through Halloran and then moved to Walter Reed for more specialized care. He was in a program focused on lip reading training being he could still speak, but Richard wanted to try his idea as well.

Sunday, the two were sitting in the rec room practicing some of the signs they were learning. Richard heard the squeaking of the wheels as a volunteer wheeled by with the library cart. He looked up and met the glance of the same girl from the library. He jumped up and knocked over his chair, he felt his face go red when he looked at Matthew who was shaking his head.

"Hi," he said, waved, set the chair right, and then shoved his hands into his pockets embarrassed at the scene he must have created.

"Hi," she signed back to him. She looked at the book at the table that the two men were sharing and understood why he had been in the library the day before.

"My name is R-I-C-H-A-R-D," he finger spelled to her the best he could and focused on her fingers as she spelled out C-A-R-O-L-Y-N. It was the most beautiful name. He raised his fingers to his mouth trying to invite her to eat with him and Matthew.

"No thank you," she signed back and tucked her head. Carolyn gave a shy wave and moved on through the room and out the door.

"That was smooth," Matthew said. He speech was slow as if he were concentrating on each word that he could not hear, but he could get the words out now.

"You were always the one with all of the charm," Richard tossed his hands up in defeat. He still was trying to remember that Matthew could not hear him and he needed to make sure he was facing him so Matthew could practice reading his lips or use the signs that they were learning.

"No more," Matthew mumbled. He felt the scars on the side of his face. He had patches of facial hair growing in around the scars.

"All of this will be behind you soon. You will be back in Tisbury taking it easy." Richard didn't want to think about it too much, Matthew's future was not going to be anything like he had planned. It was frustrating not being able to console his friend like he wanted to. Finger spelling was slow and neither could sign well enough yet. They could always jot down their messages back and forth, but Richard was warned by the staff that they wanted Matthew to learn to read lips and learn to use the signs to communicate.

They had a nice weekend visiting and too soon it was time to head back to New York.

He had a difficult time focusing on anything through the week other than Betsy's visit.

"A day leave you flat-foots," Richard tucked away his folders and waved as he left the office early Thursday and headed right to the airport to meet Betsy. He did not have to wait long until he watched the plane roll up outside the window, and the building was quickly as busy as the streets outside as the passengers came in.

"Hey gorgeous," he hugged her as she stepped in the doorway.

"Hey yourself. Wow, it is great to see you!" She missed his smile and the way he made her feel as she hugged him back.

"Let me get that for you," he took her bag and led her to the doors. "I thought we could drop off your things and then grab some dinner. You can tell me all about the picture!"

"That sounds swell, you are the sweetest of sweet." She secretly wished she could tell him...

He maneuvered through the traffic to the hotel where Betsy had made arrangements. "I am so glad you are staying downtown. The Lexington has a great band playing in the Hawaiian Room." Once inside, Betsy checked in and is escorted to her room by the bellboy. "I'll just wait down here for you. Unless you want to rest before dinner."

"No, I'll be down in a jiffy. I am still on California time, but you are probably starving." Betsy disappeared into the elevator and Richard found a chair in the lobby to wait.

'I'm a lucky guy', Richard sat thinking about the other guys who would kill to be in his shoes tonight. Betsy was beautiful, yet simple. She had changed over the past year when they first met. Not the simple girl from Wisconsin working at the docks anymore. He picked at the newspaper sitting between the chairs. Mostly the same things he read about in the office on the front page. He turned to the Entertainment section and read about a scandal involving a big Hollywood producer and an actress. He'd have to remember to ask Betsy about that.

"I'm ready." Betsy had made a quick change into a simple dress, luxurious without coming across as self-indulgent.

Richard noticed she had fixed her hair and put on some lip rouge. "I hope going out tonight isn't too much after such a long trip? I want to show you everything, but we don't have much time together."

Betsy focused on the 'together' part. She wanted the weekend to be special and memorable. "I'm sorry this trip is so short, but I will come back once the film is released and we can see it together then."

"I'm looking forward to that." He gave the maître d his name who had them escorted to their table close to the dance floor. Richard laid his hand on hers on the table after they sat down. "Is this alright?"

"I love it," Betsy said glancing down and their hands touching almost holding the other, but not willing to move. She smiled up at Richard who was oblivious as to how his touch sent chills up her back.

He looked at her and smiled again. "Are you hungry? I had a light lunch myself." She was looking at him and he suddenly felt like his chest got heavier. There was a quiet moment when he thought that there was something more to them. He just smiles and looked back to his menu.

Richard couldn't help but notice the Cape Cod Farms appetizers on the menu and wonder if they came from Matthew's father's farm. "I think I am going to order the lamb chops, what are you going to get?"

"Oh, I'll have the same. It all sounds so good."

Richard watched Betsy finish her dinner and ordered another drink. The orchestra started playing *Waitin' for the Train to Come In*. He recognizes the song as the same song they sang together in San Diego the night they met. Richard smiled at Betsy and held out his hand, "shall we?"

"This is nice," he whispered into her ear as they danced slowly. "Do you remember this song?" He ran the back of his fingers on her shoulder and back down to her waist. He could have easily kissed her right there. He held back and escorted her back to their table when the music ended. He ordered a couple of the club's infamous Hawaiian cocktails that the waiter suggested and watched the other couples on the dance floor.

They had a wonderful time, he was so glad that she had made the trip to see him, but it was getting late. Richard watched as Betsy tried to stifle a yawn. "I'll walk you to the elevator."

"Would you like to come up for one last drink?"

He couldn't resist the way she looked at him. For the first time since they met, Richard felt that things could be right for them, especially now that he was back from the Pacific, but something was holding him back. She handed him her room key so he could unlock the door for her and slid into the room. He followed her in and walked to the window where the city was spread out in front of them.

"Isn't it amazing." She was standing so close to him and handed Richard one of the glasses she had just poured and reached for her own. "Cheers." She lifted the glass to her lips, holding it with both hands and watching him from over the rim.

"Cheers," he sipped from his glass. He could feel the warmth of her body and wanted to run his hands up her arms to the back of her neck. Her lips glistened from the drink and he imagined how they must taste. He set his glass down and took her hand and moved in to taste the wine on her lips.

Betsy trembled in anticipation of the warm brush of his lips, "mmm" she purred.

Richard turned away and brought himself to his senses. He wasn't sure if they should change things between them. And she lives so far away. They were just friends, right?

"I wish I could live here." Betsy was incredibly disappointed but happy to be with him just the same.

"I want to show you Central Park tomorrow, and then Saturday, we can go to a show on Broadway. There is so much to see. Sunday, I thought we could see the Empire State Building and anything else you would like to see before you leave. He set his glass down, "it's getting late, I think I had better go. I will pick you up around 10, unless you want to wait later."

"Ten is great." Betsy could feel him retreat. What was he afraid of, what was he running from?

"I will see you then." Richard closed the door behind him and leaned against the wall outside her room. "What are you doing?" he scolded himself. He should have never gone up to her room. What if someone from the studio found out - a torrid affair like what he read in the newspaper. What if he had let himself kiss her? Would it have been so bad? He loved her, but wasn't sure what that meant.

Before he knew it, the weekend was over. He was almost relieved, he felt like he was the one acting.

Richard sat at his desk staring at the same piece of paper. He left Betsy at the airport on his way to work. He was thinking about how he held her before she boarded her plane and kissed her gently as they said goodbye. He was torn up with emotions, not sure of which direction to go.

"Spill it!" Kent added to the pile on Richard's desk. "I don't know where you are, but it isn't here."

"Girl," he shook his head. "A friend of mine came into town for the weekend." His mind wandered again, thinking about the stroll through Central Park and feeding the animals at the zoo. They really did have a wonderful time together.

"Oh, yeah? You are going to have to fill me in!" Tom Kent was young and enthusiastic. He moved a mile a minute trying to take the world in.

"Awe, don't be a drip. She's just a friend."

"Right," Tom said sarcastically. Your face has 'friend' written all over it."

"No, really. Now get back to work before the captain comes out here and sees you leaning on my desk."

"Is that who you have been going to see in Washington DC?" She must be a pretty special friend."

"No, she is not. I go to DC to see a buddy from the Army who is recovering." Tom seemed content with the answer and went back to his own desk. He didn't bug Richard about it again for the rest of the week and on Friday, Richard packed up to go see Matthew again.

Richard walked into Matthew's room to see him with a girl. He had never seen her before, but she swas crying. Matthew was writing something on the note pad very quickly. It was obvious to Richard that Matthew was agitated. He backed out the room, he did not want to disturb whatever was happening and hung out by the nurse's station.

"Who is in with Lt. Benton?" he asked the nurse sitting behind the desk.

She looked up toward Matthew's room and remembered seeing the visitor. "Not sure, but she has been here several times." The nurse went back to her file and Richard looked at the open doorway.

After a while, the girl emerged, dabbing her eyes with a handkerchief. Richard smiled at her. He didn't know who this girl was, there was obviously something that Matthew had not mentioned to him over the past year confiding in each other. Richard knocked lightly on the door, knowing that Matthew wouldn't hear it, but he did it more for the gesture. "Hi," he signed to Matthew who looked up at him from the small table in his room by the window.

"Hi," Matthew smiled. He was glad to see his friend.

Richard could see that Matthew was upset as well. He didn't want to bring up the female visitor but thought perhaps he could help in some way, if only to tell Matthew he could talk about it.

"I came in a little while ago, but you were busy." Richard was signing to him. He could see that there was a lot of writing on the note pad that Matthew kept on the table.

Matthew waved off the encounter by holding his hand under his chin and throwing his hand forward with his fingers out. Richard recognized the sign for "nothing."

"She was crying. I don't know what is going on, but I'm here if you need to talk to someone."

"I can't," Matthew reverted to speaking but watched what Richard was signing to him.

"You can't what?"

Matthew shook his head. He looked down at his hands. He felt broken and useless. "She wants me to come back home. I don't know what I want to do yet."

"Come back home? Who is she?" Richard was thoroughly confused. He never remembered Matthew talking about a sister, only his mother and father. Maybe he was married this whole time and never spilled it.

"We saw each other in High School and I saw her whenever I came home on leave. My parents sent her here, I'm sure about it. They all think I should come home and get married. She worked at the hospital on the island and thinks she can take care of me. That isn't her job, I have nothing to offer her anymore."

This was a new part of Matthew that Richard knew nothing about. He was intrigued, his raised eyebrows told Matthew that he had some explaining to do to his friend.

"I'm sorry I never mentioned Helen. I had no idea if I would make it home. I made no promises to her. She is staying in town, volunteering at the hospital while I am here, but I still think my mom put her up to it."

Richard just sat and followed what Matthew was telling him. No pressure, just someone to 'listen' to him. Nodding when he needed to, and encouraging his friend that everything would be okay.

"She's a sweet kid. We've known each other since grade school, I guess you could say we grew up together and it is just what everyone always expected." Matthew was getting tired; it had been a difficult day for him.

"Let's go eat and just forget about all of this for a little while, okay?" Richard was hungry and did not want to agonize Matthew by continuing to ask a lot of questions. They went down to eat in the cafeteria so Matthew could get out for a while.

The two picked out a table in the corner away from the dinner crowd of parents and wives visiting their son's and husbands' home from the war. It didn't seem like it then, but soon they would realize that these were the lucky ones.

. . . .

Richard couldn't help but notice Carolyn on the other side of the room eating alone. His heart beat faster just watching her. He couldn't take his eyes off of her even though he knew he was staring. What was it about this girl that threw him into such a tailspin?

Matthew touched Richard's arm bringing him back to their side of the room. "She's pretty," fanning his fingers across his face.

Richard pressed his lips together, smiled and nodded his head. "Yes, yes she is." He stood up, "I'll be right back." Richard wasn't the forward type, always very proper and a bit reserved.

Matthew watched the exchange between Richard and Carolyn. His ability to communicate using the signs that they have been learning and finger spelling seemed to be helping him. Eventually Richard came back to the table grinning.

"I have a date," Richard signed with his hands making the sign for the letter D and tapping his other fingers together. He looked at Matthew. "I'm sorry, bad timing." Richard realized he should have waited until Matthew was in better spirits as he moved his hand from his chin to his other hand, "bad."

"One of us should be happy." Matthew was still pretty gloomy after Helen's visit. "But what about your weekend with Betsy, you haven't even mentioned her. How did it go?"

"Oh, you know. She's like a kid sister."

"That's too bad. I really liked her."

"Hey, how about getting you out of here for an afternoon. The four of us can go to the museum or something."

"I am not going to move in on your date, especially your first date." Matthew continued to brood. He wanted to be happy, but couldn't get past what he felt would be a handicap for him ever having a normal life.

"You know... There are a lot of people who cannot hear and they have jobs," he said glancing at Carolyn who was still sitting where he left her. "They have families, and I'd imagine they are happy.

· · · ·

It was several weeks before Richard could convince Matthew to go out. But the day finally came when Matthew did not say no and the double date was planned. Richard was able to leave early to drive to DC to pick up Matthew and Helen then they all went to pick up Carolyn by 8 o'clock.

"I just love your car Richard," Helen slid into the back seat and waited for Matthew to slide in beside her. "A dear friend of mine back home has one just like it, but I think his is a bit newer." She turned to Matthew as she settled into her seat. "You remember Joe don't you Matthew? I think he is in the Navy somewhere. Mother keeps up on all the boys. She's become quite important with the Red Cross you know."

Richard smiled in the rear-view mirror and watched Helen ramble on. She was signing so fast Richard could not watch her and the road. Finally, he parked in front of the Brownstone which he was now becoming accustomed to after two dates with Carolyn. The first date they went to dinner and the following week he packed a lunch which they ate on the National mall and walked along the reflecting pool and then walked through the Lincoln Memorial. He had brushed his hand against hers as they walked and eventually wrapped his fingers around hers as she climbed the stairs. He could not let go. Her touch made his heart race every time.

Matthew and Helen were sitting in the back of the car when Richard came out with Carolyn. He held the door while she got settled and they headed across town. The music was already playing to the crowd that had gathered at Union Station where a room had been renovated for the USO.

"Isn't this great?" Richard was talking and signing at the same time. He was hoping that Matthew could at least feel the beat of the music and maybe even dance with Helen. He jumped at the first table he spotted with four open seats and sat beside Carolyn smiling.

"Crowded," Matthew signed to Richard. "Reminds me of San Diego and Betsy."

Richard glanced at Carolyn, but she was looking around taking in the scene. Betsy, what about Betsy! What was he going to do? He would have to deal with that soon or later.

Helen had been learning sign language as well over the past six months. Ever since Matthew's parents told her what happened to Matthew and that he would never hear again. She knew she had to do everything she could to help him. "Isn't this a scream? I've heard about these dance clubs, but I have never been before. Have you?"

"No," Carolyn signaled with two fingers closing in on her thumb. "I haven't." Carolyn was watching Helen's hands and the activity around them. She could feel the beating of a drum and occasionally the vibration from some of the other instruments. She was getting used to being around people socially again.

"I know about music; I was in the band in school. But it was more important for me to study nursing when the war broke out, don't you think?" Helen always rambled on about something.

Richard wasn't sure and that he wanted Matthew to get more involved. He wasn't sure yet what to think of Helen. Matthew liked her, so he would wait and see. Anyways, it was Matthew's choice not his. Richard looked at Helen as he took Carolyn's hand to go dance. He was hoping that Helen could encourage Matthew to do the same. It was a slow song, something they all could manage he hoped as he watched from the dance floor as Helen persuaded Matthew to come out with them.

Matthew held her and tried to move with her, he looked around at the other couples laughing and dancing. He couldn't do it. This was not normal for him any longer and ran from the floor.

Richard watched what was happening and pointed it out to Carolyn. He took her hand and led her to the door. "There they are," he motioned. He saw Matthew heading down the street toward where Richard had parked the car and Helen chasing after him. Her cries for him to wait were left unheard.

· · · ·

Richard jumped up the front steps to the front door, he noticed the dark clouds moving in and was glad they were staying in tonight. He knocked on the landlord's door and she took him up to Carolyn's apartment. He left the door open as he walked in, not sure how her landlord felt about men being there.

"I think I'm early." He looked around the cozy room. She had invited him to dinner instead of going out again. The dance last night was nice, but they would work on getting Matthew out again on another weekend. The four hour drive every weekend was exhausting. The apartment on the second floor at the front of the house had a small kitchen area with an equally small table and two chairs. The living room was a circular shape, lined by several windows with simple white curtains. He could feel the light breeze coming through.

Richard walked over to the easel set up by the window and admired the pencil drawing of a pair of hands. He noticed that the index fingers were hooked together. He did the same with his hands as he looked and the picture. He turned to Carolyn repeating the sign he knew as "friend."

"Yes, it is you. My friend."

Richard reached out and Carolyn walked into his arms. He lifted her head from his shoulder so he could see her face, the pale white skin and the faint freckles on her nose. He felt the pull and the warmth, he could barely breath. He wanted to just hold her and touch her cheeks that were so soft on the tips of his fingers, and those lips with just a hint of added color.

The smell of something burning sent Carolyn running for the kitchenette. "It's ruined," she signed.

Richard walked up behind her and looked at the slices of black silhouettes of the fish she had forgotten on the hot pad. "It's okay," he signed waving his hand. Carolyn looked heartbroken, he looked around and suggested cheese sandwiches. "Have you ever made fried cheese sandwiches?"

"No," she pouted. "You can show me."

Richard buttered a couple of slices a bread and showed her how to layer the cheese and cook it in the pan. "See, it's easy and really good." Richard noticed the lightning outside getting closer. The storm was moving in and suggested they close the windows and they sat at the cozy table to eat. He laughed as the cheese dangled from Carolyn's lips down to her chin.

"Let me get that," he motioned and reached out to wipe the cheese away and brushed her chin. His fingers lingered on the ends of her blonde hair sitting on her shoulder. They were having a nice evening sitting and laughing.

Carolyn made a cute clicking sound when she laughed, mostly at Richard when he signed something incorrectly.

They eventually moved to the couch and Richard told Carolyn about Guadalcanal and what happened to Matthew.

"You were hurt too?" Carolyn wondered. She had wondered, most men their age where overseas these days.

"I did. That same Jap plane that burned Matthew so badly took a chunk of my leg. The doctors fixed me up pretty good, but it will never be the same. This leg landed me a desk job." He patted his leg where the wound had healed. "There are so many still out there, every day they..."

Richard jumped at the clap of thunder followed almost immediately by a flash of lightning. The whole Brownstone shook and Carolyn screamed as the lights went out.

"Hold on, hold on," he called out to the darkness and deafness. Richard was feeling around for the matches by the stove and the candles he had noticed earlier.

Carolyn was crying.

He could hear her sobs and he finally was able to light a candle and hurried back to where he left Carolyn. He set the candle down on the window sill and held her as she shook and sobbed. He had never seen anyone so frightened by a storm.

She pushed back, her eyes wide and searching. "Are there planes?" She was signing frantically. "The bombs are coming!"

"No, no. There are no planes and no bombs. It is a storm, thunder and lightning." He tried to reassure her and comfort her, but confused by her reaction.

"I thought they were bombing us. It was so terrible, it reminded me..."

Richard focused on what Carolyn was telling him. He had no idea what this innocent, young girl had been through. They had never 'talked' about her past. "No one is bombing us. Carolyn, you are sitting here with me, you are safe."

"After my parents were killed in an air raid in Paris, and we never found my little brother. There was no news whether he was alive or if his body was ever found buried in the rubble. I lived with my grandmother in the 9th Arrondissement. Most of the apartments in that area were unharmed. My grandmother sent me here two and a half years ago to go to school, and away from the war."

"I am so sorry." Richard realized that the thunder storm resembled the bombings in France that she had lived through.

He lit another candle and realize that it must be getting late, but he did not want to leave especially with Carolyn still so rattled by the storm making the memories so vivid. "Tell me about her."

"Grandmother was an actress, she had a beautiful apartment, charming furniture, papered walls with grand paintings. I especially loved the silk scarves from her admirers. My room had a wonderful vanity of dark wood and a decorated mirror, she told me the canopy bed was magic. Grandmother let me try her perfumes and oils sometimes. We would walk down the streets as if nothing had ever happened. But, every time I saw the German soldiers sitting at the cafes with their tea, I wanted to kick at them for killing my parents. Grandmother told me the things they would do to those who resisted, but I despised them!"

Richard sat in amazement. He had seen action, but not in the city settings only the jungles and beaches. "How did she get you out?"

"Grandmother was afraid for me. The neighbors of my house pulled me out of the rubble and delivered me to the hospital. She took me in when I was allowed to leave, Grandmother sat with me every day while I got better. My broken arm healed but I still cried for my parents. The windows of her apartment were covered in heavy black cloth and when the planes came, she would take me down to the basement with the others. I could feel the building shake and the lights blink, just like tonight."

"Tonight was just a bad storm. We have them sometimes, but not too often. You are safe here."

"It wasn't safe there anymore. There were men impersonating police and committing crimes, you didn't know who to trust. My school was closed and taken over by the Germans. The electricity would often go out, and sometimes the water and gas would go off as well. Grandmother worked a plan with someone for me to come to America."

"Did you lose your hearing when you were hurt?"

"No, I was born without the ability to hear. I went to a special school there. Now I go to school here at Gallaudet University and work at the library and the hospital when I am not in school. Grandmother sent me with all of the money she could get without anyone getting suspicious. But that money is almost gone. She had someone from the school meet the ship when it came in to New York."

"And you are studying art." Richard looked over at the easel and the drawing she had made.

"Yes," she smiled at him. Her face glowed in the candlelight and she had calmed down.

Richard cupped her chin in his hand and lifted her lips to his. They were warm and soft and gentle. He moved back and looked into her amazing blue eyes. The sparkle was back and he knew she would be okay just as the lights came back on.

"I had better get going, its late." He smiled and moved to look for his hat, then moved in to kiss her again.

Carolyn stepped back and looked at the door where her landlord was standing.

"Is everything okay up here?" She asked.

"Yes, ma'am," Richard said to the same lady who had showed him Carolyn's apartment earlier. She was wearing a pink housecoat now and had curling ribbons in her hair. "I was just getting ready to leave."

"I can see that," she shot a disapproving look to Carolyn.

"Goodnight," he waved and grinned at Carolyn. She had calmed down by now and he knew she would be okay.

. . . .

He walked through the halls still feeling the excitement from the night before. Richard turned into Matthew's room and found him writing a note.

"Good morning."

"Yes, it is morning," Matthew was sarcastic and bitter this morning. Although, it seemed his natural repose these days.

"I had the most amazing time last night. But get this... Carolyn is from Paris and survived the German bombings before her grandmother sent her here."

"Yeah, Helen said something about her being from Europe, but never elaborated." Matthew set the notepaper he was working on aside so he could watch Richard.

"It was crazy man. That storm blew her away, scared the hell out of her. She has been through a lot. What were you working on?"

"Sending a telegram to my folks. I'm going home."

"That's great news." Richard shook Matthew's shoulder.

"What's great about it. My dad thinking nothing has changed, everyone looking at me - poor Matthew..."

"You are the only one saying poor Matthew. You are going home! You're alive! We made it through that hell. When are you going to be thankful for what you have? You have a lot to be grateful for. Come on, let's take a walk." He waited for Matthew and headed out of the room. "When are you heading out?"

"In a few weeks. I was letting the folks know."

"Hey, I was thinking about taking Carolyn to the island. How 'bout I pick you and up and drive you home and we can hit the beach, you know, have some fun."

"They have a bus to take me home."

"That's a drag! Let me drive you."

"I guess, if you insist. You can keep my father from pressuring me. He thinks that I am going to be able to help him on the farm."

"Why wouldn't you? Why can't you go home to your family and help your father who is doing so much for the war effort?"

"I'm useless Richard! I can't hear! He slapped his index fingers together and pointed to his ear. "You don't understand!" He dropped his hands as they turned into the Critical Ward.

"I think it is you that doesn't understand!" He watched Matthew scan the room and look away. "They all think that you are the lucky one."

"I'm lucky that the only time I can hear is in my nightmares? The sound of that plane screeching toward us, that won't go away? The burning of my face and hands and trying to scream, but you can't because your head is exploding?" Matthew realized that he was yelling. He looked around the room while the men that could, watched him. He ditched the scene that he had just created and headed for the area outside.

Once Richard caught up to him, he tried to help. There was an assistant behind them wondering if the patient needed to be sedated. "He's fine." Richard pushed the assistant away. "I've got this," and sat beside his friend.

"You're scared Matthew, I get it. I was scared, but I wasn't as bad off, I know. But I get asked everyday what happened, what it was like. People would see my cane and give me that pitiful look. I see the reports coming through the office, the number of wounded, the number that die every day! You're not the only one having to relive that day over and over. I hate what happened, but we have to move on. We both have lives to live."

It was tough love, but Richard was adamant that Matthew would be okay once he was able to accept his situation and learn to deal with it. They both went through the reassignment classes, Richard wondered if Matthew was really ready to go home.

"There are plenty of guys who need this place more than you do. Maybe getting home and getting busy will help. You're going to be fine, I'm here for you."

"I want it all to be over, I just want everything back to normal."

"We all do Matthew, we all do." Richard was able to calm Matthew down. He was getting him out for the day, some fresh air would do him good. Carolyn had to work, so he could spend the time with Matthew, he needed him.

Richard made the familiar trip to the Army hospital and then across town to pick up Carolyn. The threesome headed back to New York to spend the night and then on the road again to Martha's Vineyard. As the weeks passed, he had thought about putting in for a transfer to the offices in DC, but then that would mean being eight hours from home, not that he visited often.

"I don't know if your father mentioned to you, but the Navy commissioned an airbase north of you. It has three runways now and a lot of air traffic. They have a few gunnery targets and planes running training flights. I thought you would want to know being it is so close to your farm." Richard was concerned that the planes flying overhead could be unnerving for Matthew.

"He said something about it in his letter." Matthew sat in the car for the majority of the trip staring out the window.

"Let's go stand on the platform," Richard suggested getting out of the car while crossing on the ferry. They had made the long trip home.

"I didn't know they made boats to carry cars," Carolyn smiled and tied a scarf over her hair as the wind tried to blow it away.

"We live on an island. We all grew up here."

"And you are childhood friends?"

"Matthew and I met in the Army. We went through basic together and sailed to Guadalcanal and served together.

"I missed that smell," Matthew gestured taking in the salt air.

"Same here. The salt air, fresh cut grass or the pine trees."

"I like the smell of coffee at the cafe in France." Carolyn smiled.

"You will have to share that with me sometime." Richard pulled her in closer and pointed to the island coming into view. "To the left there is Oak Bluff where my parents live. We are going to dock at Tisbury and then drive about ten miles to West Tisbury where Matthew's parents live. Then back up to Oak Bluff."

"Are you sure your parents won't mind my coming."

"Oh, they'll love having us there. I don't know how much they get out anymore. Come on you two, we are about to pull in." They piled back into the car and he waited his turn to drive down the ramp, onto the dock, and onto the road.

"Here it is, turn here." Matthew tapped Richard's shoulder and directed him from the road to the entrance of the Benton's ranch.

Helen was the first to come down the porch steps to meet them, "they're here." Matthew's parents were close behind.

"Welcome home!" Helen had been showing Matthew's parents some of the basic signs to communicate with their son.

"Hi mom, hi dad." He used his voice and hugged each of them.

"Welcome home son," his mother cried.

Matthew's father wrapped his big, muscular arms around him, "you look great boy, just great." He smiled as Matthew introduced Richard and Carolyn.

"I made lunch for everyone, come in and sit down and tell us about the trip."

Helen took Carolyn's arm and was quick to fill her in about Matthew and his family. "Matthew's father is a major supplier for the Army. They own a lot of land here on the south end of the island. He is very important now you know."

Matthew smiled at Richard; he was used to Helen's stories.

"We have the cutest little shops dear. I hope you brought your swim suit, oh probably not with where you're from. We can make sure you get one, they have to latest styles, almost shameful."

Carolyn smiled at Helen and looked at Richard nervously. She wasn't used to so much activity and attention.

"You sit here darling," Matthew's mother was motioning for Carolyn.

"Mother Benton and I made cucumber sandwiches. I hope they are like the ones you had in France. I told them all about your horrific experience over there and how you came to America."

"Carolyn is about to graduate from Gallaudet University with an Art degree." Richard smiled at Carolyn as she bit into her sandwich and smiled back.

"It must have been awful for you dear. The stories we hear about the terrible things happening, and losing your parents you poor thing."

"She is very strong." Richard was trying to relay what the others were saying. Carolyn and Matthew followed as best they could.

"I took art classes in high school. Mother framed one of my paintings." Helen described the sunset on the beach picture but couldn't recall actually where it was hung.

"We all had to take art classes in school. I think I have a rendition of the same scene, although you can't tell what it is." The groups laughed interrupting Helen's next homily.

"Matthew, your room is just how you left it. You let your father know if there is anything we can do to make things easier for you."

"He is going to be just fine. Won't you Matthew darling?"

"I can answer for myself," he snapped at her.

"Matthew!" Mr. Benton pointed his finger at his son. "Helen has done nothing but try to help make your transition as easy as possible. She means well, don't be rude."

"I don't need help!"

"I think we should be getting back on the road." Richard stood up and held Carolyn's chair for her, grateful they had finished eating. "Thank you for lunch. Matthew, we will see you tomorrow?"

"Yes, I am sorry." Matthew walked them out.

"Just take it easy. This is hard for everyone." He held the car door for Carolyn and looked at his friend. "They care about you. You need to help them by letting them feel needed and they'll do the same for you."

"I'm trying." Matthew waved and went back into the house to make more apologize.

Richard drove north through the State Forest past the new airfield, he wanted to see what was going on there. He pulled off on the side of the road as close as he could get without having clearance to enter the base. A plane shot out from the trees, making them both jump.

"We all are still healing."

"I guess we are," he nodded and put the car back into gear. He continued north and then cut over to the east shore.

"Pretty," Carolyn fanned her fingers in front of her face. She watched the waves come in from the ocean.

"I've missed this." Richard turned left and made his way through the neighborhood. Not much had changed that he could see. He made a couple more turns and saw the familiar grey, stone wall appear and then the small cottage style house that he grew up in.

"Come meet my parents," he hurried around the car and opened the door.

"I'm scared," the fingers on both hands were spread out in front of her chest.

"Don't be," he grabbed her hand and walked up the stone walkway to the door between the white washed pillars. He turned the brass doorknob and came face to face with his father.

"There you are. I thought I heard something." Timothy Moeller hugged his son and then gently took Carolyn's hand. "I am so happy you are here. Annette, the kids are here," he called out.

"Dad, mom this is Carolyn." Richard had already let his parents know that Carolyn could read their lips.

"Welcome," Annette said slowly; careful to look straight at Carolyn and then turned to her son. "You look tired. You're not getting enough sleep."

Richard laughed, "I'm fine mom. It has been a long drive." He flopped down on the familiar light blue-gray couch with large pink and white flowers and pulled Carolyn down beside him.

"I'll get your bags and you two get settled. Richard, your mom put Carolyn in the guest room."

"I opened the window and changed all the bedding. There was a really nice breeze yesterday when I hung the sheets out to dry. I hope you will be comfortable."

Richard can tell his mother is nervous. One, her son brought a girl home. And two, that girl is deaf. "Thanks mom," he gets up and kisses her cheek. "I'm sure it's fine." and whispers in her ear, "don't try so hard."

"I'll show you the room," Annette wipes her hand on her apron and reaches out to Carolyn. "You can rest and freshen up if you would like to."

Carolyn looks to Richard and heads up the stairs with his mother. The house is bright and airy and she notices the smell of an apple pie.

"You'll be in this room here." They stopped at the top of the stairs and Annette opened the door to the room in front of them. "That is Richard's room," she pointed out on the right. "There is a shared bathroom between the rooms, but Timothy put a lock on there for your privacy."

"Is this okay?" Richard was already back with her brown leather suitcase. He noticed the Paris sticker on the case as he set it on the bed.

"It's fine," she tapped her thumb on her chest. "Thank you."

"You make yourself comfortable," Annette smiled and nodded as Richard ushered his mother out of the room.

"We are going to eat dinner around six. Charlie's parents wanted to say hi, so I invited them over."

"Okay, we will be down in a little while. I want to unpack a few things that I brought home." He picked up the green duffle he brought up with Carolyn's bag and set it in his own room. His mom was right, everything was just like he left it.

"I'm so glad you're home," Annette watched her son from the doorway wander through his room.

"Me too mom. I know it is only for the weekend, but hopefully this war will be over soon and I can figure things out more permanently." He picked up his football pennant and a few of the spirit ribbons from the shelf. The leather family album was sitting on his desk open to the last clipping his mother had added.

"I saved all the newspaper articles and your letters. So many boys gone. I just don't understand why we had to get involved. It was their war, not ours."

"You know we couldn't sit back and stay out of this; the Japanese just forced our hand. I heard we are dropping bombs in Hamburg and things are going well in Europe. The Japanese forces are a whole other story. They are fierce."

"The rumors of all those people sent to work camps in Poland, where did all this hate come from?"

"I don't know, but let's not talk about it when the Parkers get here. They may not want to hear about it."

"You're right. I'll leave you alone for now, but come back down quickly. I want to spend some time with my son."

"I will, thanks." He dumped the contents from his bag onto the bed and hung a few things in the wardrobe. He took his toothbrush and razor to the bathroom and saw Carolyn looking out the window in her room.

"You are lucky to grow up in a place like this, so peaceful." Carolyn signed when she noticed Richard watching her.

"I guess I never really thought about it, but yeah, I am." He reached out and brushed her bangs from her face. He wrapped his arms around her and they stood cheek to cheek looking out past the inlet beyond the yard and out to the ocean.

Carolyn and Helen sat on the blanket on the soft sand. "I just love your outfit, and all the way from Paris. I would have never thought..." Helen admired the printed bikini that tied in the front and the stylish Parisian shorts. They laughed as Richard walked toward them on his hands. Matthew ran up from the water and laid down beside Helen.

"Hey," she scolded when he shook his wet hair on her.

He laughed and mussed her hair with his wet hands. "Come get in the water with me."

Richard flipped onto his feet with a thud and pulled Carolyn to the water with him. They waded into the calm, cool water. Richard raised her into the air each time a wave reached them. He hadn't played at the beach in years.

"Come on," he waved everyone in. "I want to show you all around before it gets too late."

Carolyn threw on her bathing suit cover and floppy oversized sun hat. They folded up the blankets and packed everything in Richard's car and walked up the beach.

"This is the famous Flying Horses carousel." He went up the steps in the red barn and bought four tickets for the carousel.

"I feel like a kid," Carolyn signed as they climbed onto the carved wooden horses.

Richard reached out and grabbed a brass ring as the carousel spun around. "There is an organ playing music in the middle," he described to the others. Once the ride stopped, they all hopped off and sat on the steps drinking the Cokes Richard bought.

Carolyn noticed the number of older people using sign language. "There are many deaf people here."

"Martha's Vineyard had a long history, there is a hereditary trait here so a lot of people sign whether they are deaf or not. I had a great-grandfather who was deaf."

"I like your home very much."

"I'm glad. Here I got this for you," and handed her the brass ring from the carousel. He gave her a casual kiss. When he saw that the others weren't looking, he added a more serious kiss, and wrapped his arms around her, rocking from side to side.

. . . .

Richard hated to leave Carolyn at her brownstone, but he had to get back to New York and back to the war. He thought about her the entire ride home, and all week. He sat in his apartment alone at night thinking of her and all day at the office.

He listened to the radio and occasionally went to see a movie with some of the guys from his new unit in the Quartermasters. The news reels showed scenes from Italy and the German evacuation of Sicily, which only made him think of the men he left in the Pacific.

The news in the office was the same, supplies shipping out of the New York harbor. Paperwork for the belongings of the deceased being sent home to their families.

"All these pictures coming out are about the war," Decker walked over with the latest newspaper. "They won't let me see any action other than a picture show."

"They're afraid you'd shoot at the wrong side," Kent teased him.

"Your glasses are thicker than my Coke bottle. Imagine if you lost them." Richard held two empty bottles to his eyes. "You'd shoot your own fool head off never mind anyone else."

"Hey, here's a scoop." He laid the paper on the desk for the others to see. "Cast and crew to appear next Friday at the Marquis Theater for the premier of War Bride."

"I know, I'm going," Richard blurted out absently.

"What? Spill it. How does a sap like you land such a gig?" Kent was sitting on Richard's desk now staring down at him.

"Yeah, what gives? How come you didn't invite us?"

"I don't know, Betsy just called me the other night to let me know." Richard continued to act nonchalant about the event.

"Listen to him. Betsy just called me the other night." John Kent mocked him, strutting around the room, straightening an imaginary hat and twirling a cane. "Mr. High Society just forgot to tell us that he is going to a major motion picture premier."

"Can it!" Richard tossed the paper back to Decker. "She's a friend."

"Okay, then set me up with her." John kneeled at Richard's desk.

"Look at this picture. She's a looker." Decker whistled and showed Kent the article.

"I can't get you in, but if she has time maybe we can meet for dinner. I don't know what her schedule is going to be like. I'm not even picking her up at the airport, she is flying in with the rest of the cast."

"Where are they staying? Maybe you can get her to come down to the bar for a drink."

"Maybe, I'll ask. Now get back to work"

"Yes, sir!" Decker snapped to attention and saluted the 2nd Lieutenant.

• • • •

Richard was glad that he had his Dress Uniform cleaned. There were a few military social events, but tonight was really special. It was Betsy's big night! He walked up the steps and through the archway into the Astor Hotel. He took in the huge chandeliers and the red velvet chairs. "Would you ring Betsy Hawkins for me please?" Even the concierge's desk was immaculate.

"Hey soldier." She walked up behind him and was dazzling in her exquisite evening gown. She floated through the room in the silver satin fabric that shimmered as she moved.

"Wow," is about all he could mutter while taking her in. The dress molded to her body, the lights bouncing from the rhinestones and sequins. "You are amazing." He kissed her as she handed him the matching satin wrap.

"Thank you. You look handsome all dressed up. Oh, it is good to see you, I missed you so much." She rubbed lip stick from his bottom lip. "There is a car outside for us."

"Let's do this," he held his arm for her and they jumped in the car and headed to the theater.

"We could have walked for how close the theater is." He could see the spot lights shooting across the sky between the buildings.

"Look at the crowds." Betsy clapped with excitement. She waited for Richard to get out, took his hand and followed him from the car to the barrage of flashes from the press.

"I've got you," he put his arm around her waist and led her down the red carpet lined by stanchions.

"Isn't this amazing," she waved to the crowd and spun around once they made it through the glass doors.

He could barely see, but followed along as the usher met them. "You had better get used to it, you're a star now." He couldn't help kissing her in all the excitement. There was another flash from a photographer, they smiled and laughed.

The usher led them to the rows reserved for the cast.

"Is that..." Richard tried not to point out the leading lady.

"Yes. She's kinda rude and standoffish. Not many people like her. She is a wonderful actress though."

"I guess you work with her and know." He was in a festive mood. He sat beside Betsy and waited for the show to start. He squeezed her hand during her scenes, laughed, and found himself welling up with tears at the end. Unfortunately, the story line would hold true to many in the service but it was a great show and the crowd broke into applause when the curtain closed over the giant screen.

"You were swell, Betsy! Simply wonderful. I can't get over it, you were up there on the big screen." He moved with Betsy and the rest of the crowd out of the theater.

"You were beautiful Betsy." Someone met them in the hall and kissed her cheek. "Are you coming to the party?"

"Yes, we'll be there," she waved as the man rushed away shaking hands and kissing cheeks as he walked through the room. "That was the producer. He is fantastic."

"You are the one who is fantastic!" Richard held onto her tightly afraid they would get separated, but they finally made it outside to the lively crowd waving autograph books and calling out to the stars.

A reporter stopped Betsy along the barriers between the red carpet and the crowd. "What did you think of the show?"

"I thought it was just wonderful," she glowed and answered the next question posed to her. "My name? Betsy Hawkins, I played Ann."

"We know. You sing like an angel."

"Thank you. Thank you so much."

"Good luck kid," and then he moved on to the next actor.

"I've smiled so much my face hurts," Richard massaged his cheeks when they finally made it to one of the cars taking them back to the Astor. The after-party was being held in the Garden on the Roof at the hotel.

"Are you having fun?" She glowed under the silk covers and lattice weaved with ivy bordering the rooftop.

"Sure, I enjoy whatever makes you happy."

"Really?"

"Sure sweetie." Richard handed her another drink from the waiter who walked by with a tray of champagne. "Let's go dance, I want to dance with a movie star."

He noticed that her dress opened on the sides showing off a sexy pair of legs. He could see the silhouette of her body when the lights behind her hit just right.

"I think you're drunk," she giggled a misty-eyed laugh and moved her body to the music.

"I'm not drunk," he tried to convince her. He could barely see clearly, and the party was loud. At some point he couldn't tell if he was dancing or stumbling around the room. It all eventually was spinning together.

"Damn," Richard jumped up from the bed. He was fully clothed laying on top of the covers with Betsy sleeping quietly beside him. His head was pounding. He went into the bathroom and splashed some water on his face and ran his wet hands through his hair. 'Moeller, what are you doing,' he scolded himself.

"How are you feeling?" Betsy was propped up on her elbow watching him when he came out of the bathroom.

"Like a big drip. I don't remember coming up here."

"A few of us staggered up in the wee hours. I'm starved," she jumped up and slipped into the dressing room and came out shortly in a simple green dress with a scalloped button front. She adjusted the fashionable hat and was ready to go again.

"Do you go to parties like that often?" He rubbed his temples and groaned.

"I've been invited to a few social get-togethers, but this was my first cast party." She was trying not to laugh at him.

"I don't know how you do it." He scanned the room to make sure he had everything and they headed to the elevator.

"They have several dining rooms in the hotel unless you would rather go somewhere else."

"Here is fine, I'm hungry too." The elevator doors opened and they stepped out into the room. Everything was polished and high-class. There was a flash of light, too bright for him to bear with the hangover he had.

"Thank you miss Hawkins." The reporter rewound his camera and moved on.

"I guess I have to get used to this..."

"I don't know if I could handle the constant invasion of privacy. I guess this means you've 'made it.'"

Several people greeted her while they made their way to the restaurant. "Good morning, Miss Hawkins. Table for two?"

Richard sat down after Betsy, rearranged the silver forks and waved for a cup of coffee. "Coffee?" he asked her.

"I think I will need more than one."

"When do you have to leave?" He sipped the hot coffee, added a touch of cream and took another revitalizing sip.

"We fly to Chicago this afternoon for their premier tonight." She reached out to his hand. "You are going to have to come out to California so we can spend some time together."

"Not me," he shook his head. "I served my time out there." He watched as Betsy's expression changed. "Don't get me wrong, I'd love to come out to Hollywood, but I'm done with the military base and hospitals out there."

"Why do you think of me as a sister, can't you for once think of me as a dame?"

"Because you're no dame and you deserve someone who can help you to follow your dreams."

They ordered Eggs Benedict and ate in silence. Betsy signed the check when it came.

"I'll get that," he reached for the bill.

"Don't be silly, the studio is paying for everything. I sign and walk away. Isn't it great?"

"I guess, but it doesn't seem right for you to buy my breakfast."

"I didn't." She closed her purse and stood up. "Now, you get some rest today. I have to go pack my suitcase and meet my group for our flight."

"I didn't realize it was so late," he looked at his watch. "I guess I need to let you go." They stood in the foyer while the bellman hailed a cab for him. "Thanks for the great evening. I'm sorry I was such a drip last night."

"You were a great date and a perfect gentleman." She handed him his hat and he held onto her hand.

"Betsy. I don't know where we are going with this..."

"Don't," she interrupted. "Let's not spoil anything."

"But I don't want you to wait for me. I don't think you should." He was thinking about Carolyn and thought I owed it to both of them to be honest.

"Your cab is here, you better go." She kissed his cheek and wondered if she would ever see him again.

He decided to ride the train to DC the next weekend to see Carolyn. He did not feel like driving and he could walk or take a bus practically anywhere he was going to go. He had a difficult week; his weekend with Betsy was all over the papers and he was the butt of a lot of jokes. He had been called 'high toned, big shot, and a Hollywood snob' too many times, he nearly lost his temper once with Decker and felt badly about it later. He was looking out at the rain that was leaving little streams of water, catching the wind on the window and cascading backward. Inside he really wished that he had shared his feelings with Betsy. It was obvious that she felt differently about him that he did for her. And he should have told her about Carolyn.

"When did she move from friend to other?" He asked himself. "Hi," he waved and smiled going through his head what his conversation with Carolyn will be like. "Oh, her? She's an old friend. I've mentioned her before, right? We met in California when Matthew and I were stationed there. Sure, you can meet her sometime. She's like the sister I never had."

He walked through the front door and knocked on the landlord's door. "Hi, can you take me up to Miss Lagaisse's room?" She had no other way to call out to Carolyn than physically go upstairs.

"I don't know what you did," she shook her finger at him. You soldiers are bad boys. You make that girl cry for days."

"Is she here?" This couldn't be good.

"I think she is still at work," she responded in her thick accent.

"The hospital or the library?"

"Zee library today." She shook her head at him, he didn't stick around long enough to get the lecture that was coming.

"Excuse me," he nearly toppled over the group coming out the doors when he reached the library. He hurried to the desk, "can you tell me where Carolyn is?"

"Upstairs, probably returning books to the shelves."

"Thanks." Richard took the steps two at a time no matter how much it made his leg hurt, he wanted to see her. He wanted to make sure she was okay. He found her loading a stack of books from a table onto a cart. He looked at her and she looked away. "Wait," he signed.

"I'm working Richard." Her sign for his name was the letter R, crossing her fingers and holding them over her heart. She looked at her hand and looked down.

"Look at me," he moved in front of her and pointed his fingers at his eyes.

"No," she snapped. "I trusted you!" She clasped her fists and shook them together.

"You can trust me."

"No, the newspaper explained it. You slept with the movie star."

"What?" He was floored. He wasn't expecting that. "Wait a minute."

Carolyn moved around the table, picked up another book and placed it on the cart. She pulled a newspaper from the cart and shook it at him. "Trust you?"

The sound of the paper skidding across the table at him seamed loud compared to the silence of the library. The slapping of each of their hands as they signed and the clicking noised Carolyn made when she was expressing herself echoed in the room.

"Oh, my." He hadn't seen the picture she threw at him. The flash when he and Betsy left the elevator the morning after the premier. Betsy was in fresh clothes and he was still in his dress uniform; although, a bit disheveled. "This isn't what you are thinking. I would never..."

"You spent the night with her! I thought you liked me."

"Can we go talk? I need to talk to you." This wasn't going at all like he planned. Richard ran his hand from his forehead through his hair. "Please."

Carolyn was crying by now, but nodded her head. She would let him explain. They left the library after she checked out and walked across the street to the park.

"Betsy," he began once they found a secluded bench under the trees. "Betsy is a friend, just a friend. She invited me to the party for the film she is in." He signed slowly so he made no mistakes. "There was a party at the hotel, I drank too much. I woke up in her room." He watched the tears start again. "I was in my uniform," he tried to assure her. "Nothing happened. I would never do that."

"You kissed her." Carolyn had seen the other pictures as well, the one on the red carpet going into the theater.

"I have, but not like I kiss you."

"My grandmother had a lot of male friends. I'm sure she kissed a lot of them."

"Yes, yes. Just like that." He was feeling better about this.

"I understand."

"I hope you do." He lifted her chin and smiled trying to get even a small grin from her. "I realized that day that," he crossed his arms over his chest and pointed to her. "I love you."

"I love you too," she signed. "I love you so much, and I love your home and your friends."

"I want you to come back to New York with me." Richard was inspired and excited. It was crazy, but it was right - he knew it.

• • • •

Carolyn graduated from Gallaudet University and prepared to move to New York. She was going to travel by train to meet Richard at the station. He was on a three-day leave; it was all he could get and was afraid to ask for any more than that. All of her belongings fit into her suitcase and a steamer trunk that came with her from France and a leather portfolio with her drawings. She was ready other than sending another telegram to her grandmother, the last was still unanswered.

The couple arrived in Oak Bluffs and were immediately thrust into the final planning stages. They barely had time to catch their breath before the pre-party at the Moeller's small house. Timothy Moeller borrowed a surplus parachute and constructed a makeshift tent in the backyard with plenty of tables and chairs.

"My little boy is getting married." Annette beamed with pride.

"Mom, it looks great." He had each of his favorite ladies, one on each arm. "I don't know how you pulled this off with the rationing."

"A lot of help! It wasn't like you two gave us a lot of time to plan this for you two love birds."

"Mom is thrilled that her wedding dress fit you," he translated for Carolyn.

"I am glad too, thank you. I was having a difficult time finding a dress. This war has affected everything." She felt a glimpse of sadness.

"You just consider Timothy and me as your parents for now on." She hugged her future Daughter-in-law. "Now scoot you two, I have things to do and our guests are going to start arriving."

"Where do you want this punch?" Mr. Parker walked in with gallons of punch.

"How are you?" Richard helped him with the containers and pumped his hand. "Thank you for coming."

"Glad to be here. Charlie would be so happy for you."

"Thanks, we all miss him."

"How are you feeling? The leg healed?"

"I'm doing well, thank you. I feel bad working at a desk knowing what Charlie and the others went through."

"You did your part, and still doing your part and don't think otherwise." Mrs. Parker came up behind them.

Matthew and Helen showed up and a few of Richard's old friends that could make it. The men his age were mostly overseas.

"Your ring is just beautiful," Helen admired Carolyn's ring. Richard's CO gave him the name of a relative for a good deal on a ring. Luxuries were hard to come by, but Carolyn was thrilled when he gave her the diamond and gold buttercup engagement ring.

"Isn't it lovely," she cherished the Victorian style ring. It reminded her a lot of her grandmother and her jewels.

"My friend Clare got a carat from her fiancé. He a pilot over in Europe. He is always sending her the prettiest things." Helen rubbed her right hand covering her left fingers. "Matthew just hadn't gotten around to it yet."

"He will. He loves you."

"I know," she laughed convincing herself that she and Matthew were next.

"You're bunking with me tonight," Matthew shook Richard's hand. He was so excited when he read Richard's letter, he intended on keeping tabs on the groom.

"That's the plan. Mom said I could not stay here with Carolyn in the next room. She isn't taking any chances on us seeing each other before the wedding."

There were a lot of stories shared through the night about Richard as a kid. He left out the translation on some of the antics from his past, unless someone else was right there to communicate with Carolyn.

She had been reading lips for twenty years, but her English was a bit different from what she was exposed to now.

"See, I told you that you are bad." Carolyn teased Richard. They were finally alone. His mom and Mrs. Parker were finishing the dishes in the kitchen. Richard hummed a slow tune against Carolyn's cheek so she could feel the song with him.

"We have this for the rest of our lives," he nibbled her bottom lip and moved in with more intent. They held each other for several minutes.

"Time to go," Matthew tapped Richard's shoulder.

"No, you go away." He batted at Matthew.

"Your bride needs some sleep, you two have a big day tomorrow." He pulled Richard away as he kissed Carolyn one more time.

"I love you," he held her hand as long as his outstretched arm could reach. "Good night."

"You two stay out of trouble," Annette took Carolyn's hand and sent the boys out the door.

"Thank you for tonight Mrs. Moeller."

"Annette or mom, no Misses. People will get us mixed up. Now off to bed for you too."

Carolyn changed into her nightgown and looked out the window from the bedroom. The tent cover rose slightly in the breeze and she could see the waves in the moonlight singing the stars to sleep. "Good night mama, Good night papa, Good night grandmother."

She woke with the sun floating in through the white curtains with floral eyelet embroidery. The sun shimmered and danced on the water, she put on her robe and padded downstairs to the smell of bacon.

"Just in time. Are you hungry? I made some eggs and bacon."

"Yes, this is a treat. I don't usually spend my ration tickets on bacon."

"Neither do we, but Matthew was sweet enough to bring us some. And some fresh eggs from the ranch. Do you drink coffee or tea."

"Coffee, please. I usually save tea for the afternoon if at all." Carolyn was happy that she found it so easy to communicate with Richard's parents. They took the time to learn some signs, and she could always read their lips. She also didn't mind writing notes back and forth.

"After breakfast, we will get cleaned up. You tell me how you want your hair and I will help you. Timothy is going to drive down to supervise the boys and then come to get us."

"Good," she signed with both palms up and placing the right hand over the left. Carolyn sipped her coffee and savored the deep flavor.

It wasn't that long ago that she sat outside with her grandmother at the cafe around the corner from the older woman's apartment. The Eiffel Tower rose in the distance. She loved the rich, bold taste of her coffee, it was a luxury those days, but that day grandmother said it was a day for indulgences.

The older man who had served them limped on his stiff leg, but never faltered enough to upset his tray. Ladies sat in their jackets and their smart hats. They wouldn't dare speak of the war with so many German soldiers sitting so closely. The soldiers would smoke and drink, and she watched them laugh and carry on.

That was the day. The soldiers watched as the older woman talked to the pretty young girl with her fingers. The girl was crying and seemed to be pleading with the older woman.

Her grandmother was telling her that she was sending her to America. Carolyn had grown familiar with the area; she loved her grandmother and had no plans of leaving her only relative.

Carolyn remembered the exact table with the colorful umbrella and matching fringe hanging from the edges. She missed the smells of La Mere Katherine, the perfumes in the boutiques, and the bright flowers in the planters outside her bedroom window; she missed her family - especially today. She felt the sadness for the family that she had lost, but excitement for the family she would gain in a few short hours.

Carolyn ran her hand over the checkered table cloth. It wasn't much different from the ones in Paris.

Annette waved her hand at Carolyn to get her attention. "Where were you?"

"I'm sorry," she circled her fist on her chest. "I guess I was thinking about my grandmother."

"I'm sorry. You must miss your family so much. You are our family now. Don't worry, your folks are looking down at you and I am sure they are smiling."

"Thank you." Richard's parents were so generous with her. "My new family." She hated being so alone, but she didn't have to be anymore. "Do think I could run a bath?"

"Of course." Annette hurried her from the kitchen and up the stairs. "You let me now when you need help and I'll be right up."

Carolyn cried quietly. This was supposed to be the happiest day of her life, and here she was soaking in a bubble bath about to get married and her family wasn't there, couldn't be there.

She stood in front of the full-length mirror in the dressing room of the church looking at her reflection. Her hair was pulled back and braided with light blue flowers.

"You are beautiful," Annette placed the veil on her head and pinned it in place.

"Oh, Carolyn," Helen fussed. "Richard is so lucky. Even in a borrowed dress, you look amazing. I'm sure when the time comes, I will be just as elegant. Probably something from a major designer, I'm sure. This is so exciting."

"Helen give me those flowers and get yourself out there. I hear the music starting." She shook her head, "that girl would test my patience." Annette wanted a final look to make sure everything on the dress was perfect. "Ready dear?"

Carolyn moved behind the closed doors, arm in arm with Timothy who offered to give away the bride. He tapped her arm, signaling to her that it was time.

Helen started down the aisle first after the double doors to the nave opened. Carolyn spotted Richard standing beside Matthew in front of the sanctuary, she watched Matthew smile as he watched Helen. She turned from side to side smiling to the guests in each row.

Richard could hardly catch his breath when Carolyn walked in. She was gliding down the aisle looking like a Greek goddess in long silk which floated around her with each step - toward him!

She grasped the bouquet of white lilies. The sheer ivory crepe chiffon cover was light, and breezy. The layers were connected at the neckline so the top layer flowed with every breath of air and the sheer cape draped down to the runner.

The minister led them through their vows and the exchange of rings and then Richard had a message of his own.

"I knew the moment I loved you," he signed and spoke at the same time. "I'll cherish the moment when I knew that you loved me. I promise to nurture your soul that shines through your dreams. I promise to be your compassionate partner through everything. I promise you perfect love and perfect trust." He held his fists together at his waist. "This is my sacred vow." He slid the ring on her finger.

"I know pronounce you husband and wife. You may kiss your bride." The minister interrupted their embrace and turned them toward the guests. "May I present, Mr. and Mrs. Richard Moeller."

They walked down the aisle, Richard waved to the guys from his unit that made the trip, friends he grew up with, family of friends who were overseas, and Betsy who smiled back at them and dabbed the tears in her eyes.

Even Betsy swallowed her pride and showed up. It was a difficult phone call when Richard called to explain, but she wouldn't miss her best friend's special day. She sat in the back accepting what she had known all along, Richard was her friend and she wished him nothing but happiness.

The reception was small, but elegant. Neighbors contributed there ration coupons and helped to make sandwiches. There was even a cake with a military bride and groom.

The food the and music made the reception sparkle. Even the bottle of French Champagne presented to the couple in honor of Carolyn's heritage.

They danced and mingled among the guests. Richard walked over to a table where Decker and Kent had introduced themselves to Betsy.

"Carolyn," he was hesitant but he wanted them to meet. "This is Betsy."

"It is nice to meet you," Richard translated for her. "You are as nice as Richard said." He kissed his wife's cheek for being so understanding.

"It is a pleasure to meet the woman who claimed this man's heart. He is a wonderful friend and I hope that we can all be magnificent friends for a long, long time."

"I would like that."

"Hey, can I dance with the bride?" Decker wanted his chance and stood up to lead Carolyn to the area cleared for dancing.

"Sure, if it is okay with my wife." He looked to her for affirmation. He watched the young private and smiled at the angel following the clumsy dance moves.

"Care to dance with your best friend," he held his hand out to Betsy.

"I would love to, if you think it would be alright." Betsy glanced toward Carolyn.

"It is more than alright." He led her to the floor and moved to the music. "I am glad you came."

"So am I. I was a bit shocked, but very happy for you."

"I'm sorry I wasn't more honest with you. I don't think I really knew myself how I felt."

"It's okay Richard, I understand. It is nice to see you so happy."

"I am." They danced to a tune they both remembered from their time in San Diego. Richard caught the glance of his co-worker, and excused himself. "But now I am going to dance with my wife again." He traded partners and a wink with Decker.

Richard spun Carolyn around and held her waist and pulled their clasped hands against their bodies. They moved together, Carolyn feeling the music that Richard was singing quietly. He kissed her softly, and eventually realized they were not moving any longer.

The couple looked at each other and laughed. They went back to their table, he wanted to be alone with his bride.

"Did you see that actor, Charlie Chaplin married that child? She is only 18 years old. I think it is disgraceful! To think a man of his age…" Helen, was informing Annette of all the informalities of society.

"Mom," he interrupted. "The bride and groom are going to retire for the evening. We will come by the house tomorrow before we leave."

"Everybody get your bags of rice; they are about to leave." Helen announced waving her hands to get everyone's attention.

"Congratulations you lucky guy." Matthew walked up with a guilty smirk and shook Richard's hand. "You stay in touch."

He took Carolyn's hand and hurried to the exit and down the steps lined by their guests. They dodged the waves of rice and made it to his car that had steamers and strings attached to the trunk and tin cans in tow. Richard looked back at Matthew who smiled and gave a 'thumbs-up'.

He booked a suite at the Colonial Inn for the night. They walked through the wrap-around porch and walked into the lobby still dripping of rice onto the wood flooring and checked in as Mr. and Mrs.

Richard unlocked the door to their room, pushed the door open with his foot, picked Carolyn up and carried her into the room. He closed the door softly behind them, they were finally alone in the glow of the fireplace beyond the foot of the bed.

He popped open the bottle of champagne and poured two glasses. "To the woman who just made me the happiest man alive, Mrs. Moeller."

Richard set their empty glasses on the table and braced his hands in her silky hair and removed the pins letting her hair fall to her shoulders. He leaned in and felt her breath.

She stirred and allowed herself to feel as she had never been allowed to before. She grabbed on and pulled him in. "Is this what it was like?" She asked herself.

Like the waves outside, his emotions rolled in. His mouth to hers, parting her lips. He sank in and felt her yielding to his warm fingers. He felt heat, but slowed long enough to loosen her buttons and knots holding her flesh in.

She slid her hands down his back and let the silk fall from her shoulders. She felt his heart beating, smelled the salt of the sea, and the flowers and the musk of the man she would share the rest of her life with.

Their passion taught them, and led them to places he had only imagined until now.

. . . .

They had the day to settle into his apartment. He had already moved some of his things in the dresser and wardrobe to make room for Carolyn's clothes.

"I have a surprise for you," she laid her leather portfolio on the little table in the kitchen.

"These are great." He pulled each of the pictures out one by one.

"You've seen this one. 'Friend' from when we met and became friends."

"And this one?" Richard held up the drawing. She had drawn the fingers of one hand down on the palm of the other.

"Truth is when I realized that I loved you."

"Love," he held up the next one. "When you realized I love you?" He kissed her. We will get these framed and hang them.

"I have another, but I haven't finished yet." She showed him the incomplete picture of two hands in the sign of marriage.

"These are a great gift. Thank you so much."

She brought so much life to him that he didn't even know was missing. "It is such a dark time in the world, how were they able to be so happy", he'd ask himself.

Carolyn quickly got a job at the Brooklyn Museum. She would help to catalog the works that were displayed in the halls or stored in the storage rooms. She loved the work and could get home every evening before Richard and cook dinner for the two of them. They were settling into their life together.

Carolyn was in the kitchen opening a can when she noticed her light flashing. Richard had thought it a good idea to wire a light fixture to the doorbell so Carolyn would see when someone was at the door. He remembered always having to bother her landlord in DC.

When Richard came home and found Carolyn sitting on the green couch staring out the window. She didn't see him come in.

"How was your day?" he sat beside her and tried to ask.

She turned to him and he could see she had been crying.

"What's wrong? What happened?"

"Grandmother," she picked up the telegram and showed it to him.

"Regret to inform you that Mrs. Estelle Lagaisse has passed. Letter will follow. Harry R. Jacobs." He set the paper back on the table. "I'm so sorry honey."

"I felt it somehow." She held her handkerchief to her nose. She is with my parents now.

"Who is Harry Jacobs?"

"Her attorney I believe."

"You know I would take you back there if I could. It isn't safe Carolyn."

"I know. And someday I want to show you the Arc de Triomphe, and go to the top of the Eiffel Tower, the shops, and the cafes, walk along the Seine." She cheered at the thought of sharing these things with him. "But not now, not while there is so much danger."

"You will show all of those things to me sometime, this war can't go on forever." He finished cleaning up after dinner and comforted her when he found her laying on the bed.

He tucked in beside her, curve matching curve and wrapped an arm around her. He only thought to comfort her, and wasn't expecting her to respond.

She turned to face him then closed her eyes pushing away the thoughts that she worried would haunt her through the night. She tentatively reached out to him, then led his hands to comfort her. Carolyn circled her fingers on his chest.

Richard covered her with his lips, kissing her ear lobe and moved to the crevice on her throat. He could feel her swallow and met her lips.

She needed to feel him and felt his arousal. She loosens his belt and moved on top of him. She pushed away the demons as she clutched at him, squirmed and gasped. Her life was here now with her husband to make their future, together. Her past was just memories, her family was now all gone.

• • • •

It was another week before the anticipated letter from Paris arrived. Richard looked over the letter with Carolyn but it was written in French. For once, she had to translate for him.

"A representative from our firm will arrive in New York on the date below to meet Miss Lagaisse the beneficiary for the late Estelle Lagaisse. There is a considerable investment to be sent to the only heir to the estate." She handed the letter to him.

"That's next week," he turned the envelope over to see when the letter was mailed.

They spent the weekend Christmas shopping. They planned on going to the island for the holiday. Carolyn shared stories about her grandmother, her parents, and the places in Paris.

"One summer my father took us to the sea shore, I think I was ten years old. We walked on the path down the hill to the water and played in waves and they came in. Mother set out bread and made sandwiches. We spent the week in a small town, Cannes. If we weren't at the beach we were walking through the churches. They have towering steeples, and stain glass windows."

He enjoyed watching her enthusiasm as she described the places she loved as a child.

"William the Conqueror is buried there, he was responsible for building the Abbeys. Mother said the Pope made him build them for repentance. There is a wonderful castle Chateau de Caen, with a real draw bridge. The stone blocks are nearly a thousand years old. There is cool green grass all around. I wonder how much will be left when the war is over."

"You know we were facing each other," he stated.

Carolyn responded with a questioning look.

"You were on the French seashore looking out to the west, and I was on the seashore in Martha's Vineyard looking to the east, right into your eyes. Your heart was already looking into mine."

They met Mr. Dunne, Mr. Jacob's partner at his hotel, he suggested they meet for dinner to discuss the legal matters when he arrived in New York.

Richard was glad they sent someone who spoke English; even so, he had a time of it trying to relay the details to Carolyn. The man's English was broken and mixed with his accent made him difficult to understand.

"The apartment and its contents will be preserved to the best of their ability for Carolyn to claim the property. There is a sizable trust which we are presenting you with a check."

Richard squeezed her hand in support. The whole thought of ending her connections to her home was difficult.

"We are also sending a trunk to your home address with some personal things we thought you would like to have."

"Thank you," Carolyn appreciated all that they were doing. It was hard not being able to attend her grandmother's funeral, she needed some closure. Even in her parent's passing, as hard as it was, she had been there.

"And congratulations to you two. Your grandmother would have been very happy to know you are doing so well."

"Thank you, Mr. Dunne." Richard stood and shook the man's hand and held Carolyn's chair for her. "If there is anything else you need, let us know."

"You will sign for the delivery," he told Carolyn. "But I have everything I need here." He stacked the paperwork with her signatures and placed them in his bag.

"Thanks again, and Merry Christmas."

"My pleasure." He picked up his briefcase and hat and followed the couple out of the restaurant. "I have family here, that is why I made the trip. It will be a nice vacation before I have to try to get back." He wanted to spare them the brutal details over in Europe.

• • • •

Richard was trying to finish the last requisition he needed to approve. He was in charge of distributing the money budgeted and ensure the supplies continued to flow.

"Listen to this," John walked over to Richard's desk with the latest newspaper. "*There are so many bodies of dead Italians lying in the streets. Some of them were shot down for no reason except they were walking in the streets.*" He continued to read as others gathered around. "*I saw a German shoot and Italian soldier who still had a rifle. A young man ran to pick up the rifle and he was killed too.*"

"You saw stuff like that, didn't you Moeller?"

"No, well not exactly. I was in the Pacific. What else does it say?"

"*I saw a German soldier flip a cigarette butt into the street. A young youth stooped to pick it up and he was shot. There is an absolute reign of terror existing.*"

"That's it," Decker walked toward the CO's office. "If I don't get a transfer over there this time, I'm going to walk over there myself."

"Damn kid," Richard watched him disappear behind the door. "He has no idea." It bothered him as well, sitting behind a desk. He also knew how lucky he was and finally realized no one would question his patriotism. He filed his paperwork and grabbed his coat. He was taking his wife to his parent's house for the Christmas holiday.

• • • •

The snow was just beginning to fall when they reached Martha's Vineyard. The streets were decorated with the weathered streamers crossing from side to side with tinsel snowflakes hanging in the middle. There were a few people on the streets making their final Christmas Eve purchases.

"Merry Christmas," Annette hurried from the kitchen to greet the young couple. She had even been practicing more signs and felt better about communicating with Carolyn. The more she learned, the more she realized what a beautiful, expressive language it is. She moved her hand from her cheek and cradled her arms.

Carolyn looked confused for a moment at the sign, she thought her mother-in-law suspected something.

"Welcome home daughter."

"Smells great in here mom," Richard set down the bags and packages that he carried in.

"I'm scraping together what I can to make you a Christmas dinner."

"She's been in the kitchen all day," Timothy hugged Richard and snuck in a kiss on Carolyn's cheek. "You both look good."

"It's snowing," Richard took his wife's coat and hung them on the hook behind the door.

"Just don't track it into my clean house."

"Gee, how old am I?"

"Not too old to listen to your mother!" She reached up and brushed the snow from his hair. "Your father started a fire and I'm making hot chocolate. You two sit over there and warm up. I saved the last of the tree trimming for when you made it in."

"Mom makes the best hot chocolate," he motioned to Carolyn.

"Have you seen Mrs. Roosevelt's column, My Day? She went to the South Pacific to visit those boys. They say she is 'dedicated to a better way of life for all the people of the world'. I think she has a way with people and can comfort the boys over there as only a mother can do. Says here that she went to a chapel and a graveyard on Guadalcanal. The chapel was built by the natives and given to the soldiers all decorated with a cross on top. There is a picture here with her wearing a Red Cross uniform." Timothy turned the paper for Richard to see.

"Don't bother him with talk about the war, they are here to relax."

"I remember too much about being there." He remembered too much about his last Christmas. He picked up an ornament from the box. He smiled at the memories of the glass bird ornaments with a spun glass tail, they had springs for legs so they bounce if you touched them. He clipped them onto the branch of the tree. He remembered the scolding from his mother when we were young for playing with the ornaments.

"I haven't had a Christmas tree in several years now," Carolyn watched and the tree bloomed with color. The ornaments twinkled as the reflection from the fire bounced off of them. She noticed that it sent sparkles dancing like stars on the ceiling.

"I have something for you that I want you to open tonight." Annette handed her a box with simple paper and a red ribbon tied into an elegant bow.

"Thanks mom," Richard moved to watch Carolyn open the small package.

"It's beautiful," Carolyn fanned her fingers in front of her face and pulled the Santa and Mrs. Clause from the box from the ribbon attached to Santa's hat.

"Your first Christmas ornament for your family." Annette was so pleased with the ornament she found. It was perfect for them.

"We didn't put up a tree, but we'll hang it on yours for now." Richard held a branch while Carolyn looped the ribbon around the pine needles with the ornament facing out into the room. It was the best Christmas ever!

Richard rolled over in the bed and reached out for his wife. He opened his eyes and saw the white sheets and the empty pillow with the imprint from where she had been. He threw on a pair of trousers and a shirt and opened the door quietly. He didn't know if his parents were up yet on not. He could smell coffee, so someone was up.

He stopped and admired the tree from the stairway. He has witnessed this same scene over many years, the decorated Christmas tree with the gifts waiting for him. There wasn't much this year, but he had everything he needed with her.

He filled a mug with coffee and walked around the small house and finally found her on the back porch wrapped in a wool blanket.

"What are you doing out here?" He handed her a mug of steaming coffee.

"It is so pretty," she said taking in the snow-covered trees.

"Good morning." He shaded his eyes from the sun reflecting from the ice that formed on the shore. "Is there room under there for me?"

"Of course," she opened the blanket and moved over on the wicker love seat; her legs drawn up underneath her.

"It's cold out here," he cupped the mug breathing in the steam from the coffee.

"It doesn't matter what time of year it is; it is always so pretty here."

"You like it here, don't you?"

"My second favorite place."

"And your first?"

"Where ever you are."

"Here you two are," Annette peaked out the door. "It's freezing out here. What are you doing?"

"Experiment on body heat," he laughed then explained to Carolyn what he said.

"Come inside before you catch your death. Richard, you get a fire built."

"Ho Ho Ho," Timothy bellowed from the top step.

"What are you wearing?"

"Your mother's handmade Christmas sweater." Timothy smiled and watched his son roll his eyes when he saw that Annette wasn't looking. "Careful son, I think there is one under the tree for you too."

"Don't start opening packages yet." Annette slid a pan into the oven. "There, I made cinnamon rolls and let them rise overnight. I didn't think I was going to have enough sugar, but I made do with some extra molasses."

"You are in for a treat." Richard handed Carolyn her mug that he refilled.

"I'm first," Annette hurried into the room and lifted a package from under the tree. "This is for the two of you."

They untied the ribbon from the heavy quilt that Annette had hand sewn for hours over the past month in order to have it ready for Christmas. She described each of the squares from old pajamas to Richard's favorite shirts to Carolyn. "Every time he outgrew something, I would snatch it up and tuck it away." Each patch told a different story.

"Now our turn," Richard handed a package to each of his parents.

"I picked out the fabric," Richard pointed out to his mother. "Carolyn picked out the basket.

"I love it, thank you." She looked through the wicker sewing basket with spools of colorful threads and new scissors. She planted kisses on each of their cheeks.

"This one says it is from Santa," he eyed his parents for a clue.

"Looks like someone knew you love to draw." Tears welled in Carolyn's eyes as she opened the wood case full of charcoals and paints.

"I don't know what to say, thank you." She moved her hand from her chin out toward the older couple then hugged them both.

"One more thing," Richard pulled the last gift and handed it to Carolyn. "Kodak 35, see it is the newest thing." He was so excited, and pointed out each of the camera's features to her. "You don't have to worry about opening and closing a lens, and this metal knob turns the film inside the camera so you can take another picture. It takes color pictures too, isn't it great. I wanted you to have this for when we get to go to Europe and we can photograph all the things you have been describing to me."

Annette looked worried, "You're not going to Europe are you Richard?"

"No, mom. We will go after the war is over. I want to see where she grew up, and where she went to school, and where she played as a child. And we want to put flowers on her parent's and grandmother's graves."

"You're such a strong girl." Annette patted her daughter-in-law's hand.

"One more," Carolyn tapped her pointed fingers together end to end. "I think there is something over there," she pointed.

Richard turned to look where she was pointing to. "Where?"

"I didn't leave anything over there, did you?" Annette questioned her husband who shook his head.

"I saw something behind the curtain."

"I shut the drapes last night, there wasn't anything there." Richard insisted, but got up anyways to look. Just as she had predicted, there was something leaning against the wall covered by a white sheet.

"This wasn't here... that's why you were up so early this morning!"

"Bring it here Richard, let's see." Annette cleared a space on the coffee table.

He uncovered a wooden frame with gold detailing, the frame held new hands. "You drew another picture for me."

"It's lovely dear." Annette touched the black ink. "They're so delicate and precise. You drew this?"

"She is a wonderful artist mom. You should see the others, very special gifts - each of them means something."

"Oh?" She continued to inspect the picture as Richard described the previous messages to her.

"The first one said 'Friend' from when we met and the others continued as we fell in love." He turned the frame to get a closer look. "The fingers are in the sign for the letter s, and lips of course and the outline of a woman's face. The thumb touching the lips." He looked to Carolyn to make sure he was getting it right.

"Yes," she signed.

"Next pair of hands, one covering the other. And the last here..."

"Looks like your mother telling you to be quiet, you know like, shhh." Timothy joined in, curious to what the gift really was.

"Now it looks like the hands are moving the way you blotted the ink, like a smudge. Do I get a hint?"

Carolyn moved her hands as she meant the picture to reflect. She watched as they watched, repeated and considered different possibilities.

"It says secret...?" Richard stated but questioned if he was correct.

"Yes," she smiled in the excitement as they deciphered her message.

"You have a secret," he put his arm around her. "Let me guess. You're a French Princess?"

"No," she grinned and shook her head.

"You bought me a puppy."

"Wrong again."

"Could it be?" Annette smiled a hopeful smile at the girl.

"What? What could it be?" Richard asked the women who apparently now were sharing a secret.

"Can I?" Annette asked to explain the message to her son. "I don't think it is as much a secret as it is an announcement."

"I still don't get it. Call me a dope."

"You are going to be a..." Annette held her fingers up and tapped her thumb on her forehead. "Father!"

"Me? We're? You?"

"Yes," she nodded as he scooped her up and swung her around.

"Put her down, have you lost your head?" Annette scolded her son and moved in to congratulate them.

"I'm sorry, I'm sorry," he laughed and kissed Carolyn. "How long have you known, how?"

"Congratulations you two."

"Thanks dad. What a great Christmas surprise. We're going to be parents! And, you're going to be grandparents," he laughed and slapped his father on the shoulder. "We can teach him to sail like you showed me, and play baseball..."

"Or she," Carolyn added.

"I love him or her already."

Chapter 12 COOPERATION

Carolyn flipped the pages of the Sears catalog looking at the variety of cribs and layette sets. She wanted yellow and Richard thought they should wait until the baby arrives and they know whether it is a boy or a girl.

They were moving into a larger apartment now that they needed an additional bedroom for a nursery. It was just down the street, almost identical Brownstone like hundreds of others in the area.

She's doing great mom." Richard was on the phone with his parents. They called at least once a week to check on the expectant parents. He watched his wife and winked when she looked up at him. He watched her turn the pages back and forth and stopped working on the box that he was unpacking and walked up to his wife. He could hear music through the open window from someone else's apartment.

Her figure was deceptive from behind, but it was obvious that it wouldn't be more than a couple more months and they would have to make a decision.

She caught him watching her and closed her fingers together, "what?" She blushed and glanced away as he danced toward her.

The song was slow and romantic. He placed his beer on the table and eased her up from the chair with one hand and took her in his arms. She still captivated him even as her belly continued to grow. Her face, her nose and those eyes that melted his heart. He shared the music with her as he often did when they danced cheek touching cheek. He lowered his eyes to her mouth, her full lips and swept a stray hair away with the back of his fingertips.

He tightened his arm around her waist and felt the bulge of the baby between them. He took her hand, light and delicate and swayed to the music looking deep into her eyes.

He picked her up and took her to the bedroom, the linens not even in place yet other than tossed out waiting to be addressed. He set her down and moved to stand behind her. He put his hands on her shoulders and pulled her back into him and kissed the silky skin on the back of her neck. His hands ran down her arms to her waist finding the zipper to the skirt she wore. The material dropped to the floor and unhooked the snaps of her blouse. He turned her to face him and gently lowered her to the bed following her with tender kisses. He massaged her swollen feet then moved to kiss the belly poking proudly between them and pulled his knee onto the bed beside her and stretched out against her. He kissed his way up her body stopping at her swollen breasts as his hands explored. He dared not to move on top of her, he did not want to bear any of his weight on her. Richard could feel the subtle movements of their baby as they held their hands on Carolyn's belly.

"Only a few more months and we will have our wonderful baby here." He kissed his wife and tucked her hair back behind her ear.

Richard couldn't have loved her more. Each month as she blossomed, he found her more and more beautiful. He lay beside her stroking her skin until she drifted off to sleep.

• • • •

Late Monday night in early June, he sat as his desk as the news poured in. They had been working feverishly over the past months helping to get new uniforms, jeeps, ammunition, and other supplies overseas. The requisition lists were more than anything he had seen come through his office. Everyone knew an invasion was coming, it all depended on when General Eisenhower decided to 'pull the trigger.'"

"I wonder where Decker is by now."

"If he got his way, he is in the thick of it."

They sat around listening to the radio broadcasts as D-Day was in full swing. The war was about to take a major swing to the favor of the Allies.

They listened intently to the reports from the announcers, "D Day has come. Early this morning the Allies began the assault on the north western face of Hitler's European Fortress…"

"I read that Eisenhower issued an order to be read to each of the different forces assembled."

"They do that before a major battle, to remind the men of their duty and the cause. I heard a few and gave a few, but nothing to this extent. This is the first time I have ever heard of the same order repeated to all of the troops." Richard looked at his watch.

The CO eventually called it a night and told them to go home. Richard hurried home to Carolyn. She may not know yet. She may not know that over 100,000 men just landed on the shores in France. The same shores that she spent the summers on with her parents were being taken back from the Germans.

Richard stopped and bought some flowers on his way home; this was a meaningful day for her.

He unlocked the door to the apartment and didn't see her, "Maybe she's gone to bed already." Richard opened the bedroom door and saw her curled in a ball on the floor.

"Carolyn, Carolyn," he hollered.

Her eyes were closed but he felt that she was breathing, but she wasn't conscious. He tripped on the flowers that he dropped when he ran back to the front room to call for an ambulance.

"What's her name," the police officer yelled at Richard when he didn't answer.

Richard was frozen. He couldn't move, the room was spinning with Carolyn in the center of it lying on the floor. He thought he heard birds; big birds pecking down on him.

"Soldier, stand down!" The officer tried to get Richard to snap out of it and help them.

"Sir?" He turned, he was scared and confused.

"That's better. What is her name?"

"Carolyn. Carolyn Moeller." He moved to her side, knowing he should stay out of their way, but he had to touch her, hold her hand.

"How far along is she?"

"Um, six no, seven months."

"How long has she been like this."

"I don't know, I was... I work in the Quartermasters office. We were late with all the news reports. The invasion."

They loaded her on the stretcher and lowered her down the steps. Richard tried to stay by her side but the steps were too narrow. He caught up with them and tried to get into the ambulance but was stopped mid-step.

"You can't ride with them."

"That's my wife."

"Come on Lieutenant, jump in my car with me." The officer pulled him away from Carolyn so they could close the doors.

"Where did you serve Moeller," the officer took his name from his uniform. He judged by the limp that Richard has seen some action.

"Guadalcanal." He stared ahead watching the ambulance maneuver down the street, the red light spinning through the neighborhood to the hospital.

"Bad stuff over there. Couldn't serve myself. The Army decided I was too old, so here I am on the beat every night." The officer glanced over at Richard; he was trying to distract him even a little on the drive.

"Where you from?" He honked at a car that didn't move over far enough.

"Martha's Vineyard. Do you think she is going to be okay? Why didn't she wake up?"

"Take it easy. The body takes care of itself. Those babies do amazing things to their mothers and it's amazing how it all goes back to normal."

"I guess it does." He could see the hospital now and saw that the ambulance was pulling in.

"Is this your first?" He remembered that no one else was in the apartment, but he never checks the other room.

"Hey, thanks for the ride. I'm going to get out here." Richard barely waited for the car to slow down and he was out of his seat and sprinting for the emergency entrance.

He was stopped before getting to the examination room where they took her. "You need to wait out here."

"I need to see my wife," he ordered.

"We need to get some information from you. That is how you can help right now. Let the Doctors take care of her."

He filled out the forms and sat on the hard bench waiting for someone to come out and talk to him. He held his head in his hands holding back the waves of emotions and the minutes ticked by.

He had to get up and walk around, the waiting was driving him crazy. Why didn't someone come out and tell him how she was. He walked over the phone on the counter and dialed his old number.

"Dad."

"Richard, we heard about the invasion. Your mother and I were listening to the radio just before we went to bed."

"Dad, something..."

"Richard, what is it?"

"Carolyn. She's in the hospital. The ambulance came and got her."

"Where are you?" Timothy sat up in bed and whispered to Annette that something was wrong.

"I'm at the hospital. I came home late, we all had to stay - she was on the floor unconscious. She won't wake up dad, she won't wake up."

"We're coming up there. Your mom wants to talk to you," he handed the phone.

"Richard, is it the baby?"

"I don't know mom. They haven't said anything yet. The doctors are still in with her."

"We are getting dress and driving up there right away."

"No, don't do that. I... wait until I hear something. I will call you back as soon as I can." He hung up the phone and found one of the cushioned chairs had been vacated. He sat down, and felt the panic building inside again. He gets up and starts pacing the room. He sat back down again, he was exhausted. He was being torn from one emotion to another.

"Why didn't I insist that someone look in on her? Why did I stay at the office so late? She's been through so much, why is this happening? What if I lose her, I can't lose her." He buries his head in his hands.

His mind drifted back to the white hallways in Long Beach at the hospital. One day a soldier was there and the next he was gone. Their stay was unknown, that inevitable question. So many had been lost already. Those who made it home were the lucky ones. Forever scared, but alive!

It did not seem like more than eighteen months ago. He had read letters from home for those who were unable to read their own mail. "We love you son; we are all thinking of you. Darling, I can't wait until you get home."

So many of the letters hit home for all of them. Everyone had a parent, sister, brother, friend, or lover waiting for this war to end. 'I hoped that I would never have to write a letter as this one. Your brother has been killed. None of us can believe he is gone. He was sitting in the radio tent when the first shell came in. He was hit by shrapnel in the neck and died instantly. He didn't suffer and you would be happy to know that he was writing to you at the time. Enclosed is that letter, his last thoughts of his family.'

Another time, he had helped to write a letter for a soldier lying in bed with both arms strapped in traction. "My Baby Sharon Leigh. This is my first letter to you my sweet baby. Today you are a whole month old already, and I haven't seen you or a picture of what you look like. Your father left before you were born, knowing you would be arriving soon and wishing very much to be there when you arrived. Your mother and I always wanted a little girl just like you. Most fathers wish for a little boy, but not me. I wanted a little girl, just as beautiful as her mother. I love your mother very much, and there would be nothing better in this world than to have a little girl just like her. Your daddy thinks a lot of you and wants nothing more than to come home and take care of my two beautiful ladies. Good night sweetheart, your daddy will be there for you soon."

What him made him dream of that now?

"Mr. Moeller?"

"Yes, I'm Richard Moeller." He must have dozed off and jumped at the sound of his name.

"Your wife is awake. Would you like to go see her?"

"Yes," he reached for the olive jacket that he had taken off. His tie was undone, and his face showed the time passed since his last shave.

"There is something you need to know before you go in."

Richard stopped and looked at the doctor. He braced himself.

"She lost the baby. We haven't told her, we thought maybe you could help considering her... communication problem."

"What happened?" He shook his head not understanding why, how could this happen?

"These things happen, I'm so sorry." The doctor was trying to console Richard before he went in to see his wife.

"She's very weak and still out of it. But she should pull through just fine."

Richard walked through the door and saw her laying there in the bed. She was so pale and drawn. All the expectations of motherhood and been ripped away from her. How was he going to tell her?

He walked up to the bed and kissed her forehead. There was a chair close by, he reached out and pulled it closer so he could be next to her and hold her hand. He stroked the back of her hand. Those beautiful hands that spoke to him, those hands that she drew to immortalize her messages to him.

He thought of the pictures she had drawn, "my friend." He loved her playful way of teasing him when used the wrong sign and unintentionally made a joke.

"Oh Carolyn, I have a terrible secret for you." He thought about how happy she was when she shared the news. He didn't let her order the things she wanted for the nursery, he wanted to wait to see if the baby was a boy or a girl. He didn't even know...

He felt her stir and watched as her eyes opened, looked around the unfamiliar room and met his. He tried not to look sad, but she noticed.

"What's wrong," she moved her little finger from her top lip and replaced it with her thumb.

He was about to hand her an immediate and profound change in their life together. He looked away; how can he break this news to her.

She squeezed his hand, "baby?"

"The baby is gone," he explained to her, tears welling in his eyes then sliding down his face. "I'm so sorry."

A sob escaped her, she clamped her hand over her mouth. "What happened?" She signed with a shaking hand.

"I found you on the floor. I couldn't wake you up so I called an ambulance."

"It hurt; I wasn't sure what to do. I was going to go downstairs or knock on the door down the hall. I don't remember."

"It's okay. I'm here."

They cried together until she finally fell asleep again. He watched her chest rise and fall and the evidence in her figure that she was no longer carrying their baby. They had so many plans. His parents had been thrilled about becoming grandparents.

"My parents," he jumped up to find a phone to let them know the Carolyn was okay but they had lost the baby.

"They said she may have been having early labor pains. She collapsed on the floor either from the pain or she lost consciousness from when she hemorrhaged. She lost a lot of blood. They delivered the baby and he was dead." The words caught in his throat as he said them.

"We wish you were closer to home son." Timothy held the phone so they could both hear what Richard was saying.

"I do too dad. Someday when this war is over, maybe we'll find a place on the island and move back. Until then, I am in the Army doing what I can to end this thing."

"We love you both," Annette chimed in.

When Richard came back to the room, she was awake and propped up in bed. The doctor was standing beside the bed with a nurse and the nurse was signing to Carolyn.

"You will heal and maybe even have another baby someday, but you need to wait a while until you are better."

She nodded and wiped the tears from her cheeks. "Thank you."

"You get better and we'll get you back home soon."

She nodded and reached out to Richard. "I lost the baby."

"I know." He wasn't sure what to say. Just holding her for now seemed to help. She apparently didn't remember his conversation with her earlier.

"Mom said to tell you they love you and they want us to come down soon to rest and soak up some of their healing sunshine."

"I told them that I would like to come home to bury our son."

"Our baby was a boy?"

"Our baby was a boy. I'm sure he had your amazing eyes and beautiful hair. His fingers would have been as graceful as yours when he learned to speak." He pushed her hair behind her ear.

"I would like that. I would like to take him home."

• • • •

It wasn't like he had anticipated, coming home to an empty house without the cries of their infant son. Richard helped her into bed. The doctor recommended that she stay in bed a few more days for her body to recover. He had already packed of some of the things they had bought for the baby. He didn't know how she would feel about seeing those things when she got home, so he stored as much as he could in the closet. They had time to try again.

He kissed her, gently. She was fragile needed time to heal mentally and physically. All they had wanted was to hold their baby in their arms. Why was this happening to them? How much did she have to go through, how much did she have to lose?

Richard sat watching his wife sleep, his throat tightened as he tried to blink away the tears. He finally let them flow as he choked on the sobs escaping him. He had never felt the pain of loss until now.

Richard didn't know which would be more difficult. But after a week in the hospital and several more resting at home she was beginning to get up and around the house. Their neighbors down the hall a Lieutenant and his wife from Iowa, Bea was going to check in on Carolyn now and then.

Bea and Carolyn went to the movies together when Carolyn finally agreed to get out of the apartment.

"There is a movie playing down the street that I read about. Do you go to movies? I mean, being you can't hear do you like to watch? We can do something else."

"I will go to a movie with you, and no, I don't typically go see them."

"Meet Me in St. Louis is playing. It is a wonderful movie with Judy Garland. We could eat lunch at the deli and still be home before the guys get home.

"I like that idea." Carolyn smiled.

The two women walked down the street for their afternoon out. The headline on the paper on the newsstand caught Carolyn's eye. "Liberation of Caen" it made her smile.

· · · ·

"It is sunny and warm today," he signed when she turned around. "Why don't you take a break, let's go for a walk in the park." He liked that she was drawing again.

"That's a great idea. Give me a minute and I'll be ready to go. There are some things I want to pick up at the drug store too."

They walked as far as the benches by the pond and sat so Carolyn could rest.

"Are you sure you are okay? It is so hot out here."

"I'm fine, it is nice to be out."

"Have you thought anymore about going back to work? It has been two months; it might be good for you."

"Yes, I feel better but my heart still hurts," she held her hand to her heart.

"My heart hurts too," he bought two ice cream cones and walked back to her on the bench. "Eat it quickly, this heat is going to melt the ice cream."

He licked around the edges of his cone and looked up at the sky. The deep blue was being covered by more and more clouds. "I saw a weather report at work, I'm afraid that this heat is going to pull those storms north."

"I don't like storms."

"I know, but remember that it was a storm that brought us closer together." He smiled and wiped his hands on his trousers. "We are going to live through a lot of storms, but we will always have each other."

They walked over to Central Park Zoo and watched the children running around the legs of their parents. Richard glanced at Carolyn to see her reaction, she only smiled. Her expression gave nothing away to what she was feeling.

She took her husband's hand, "I'm fine, really."

They walked up the paved walks, between the cages of monkeys.

"I know, but these monkeys smell awful." He looked up again as the clouds continued to move in. They could be in for a heck of a storm tonight.

Two boys skid past them tossing popcorn bombs at each other. "They coming for us, blast them," Richard heard the boys as they reenacted a battle they probably read about.

"Let's head back, I don't want to tire you out." He led her back through the park with his arm around her waist.

The wind picked up and although the heat wasn't subsiding the skies were getting darker and darker. By the time they walked out of the drug store on the corner, things had changed even more. The wind was sweeping across the sidewalk and the striped canopy over the stoop flapped intensely. The sign propped up on the sidewalk fell over with a thud.

"I think you were right about the storm." Carolyn held onto her hat as a gust of wind nearly swept her right off of her feet.

They laughed and hurried arm in arm toward their apartment. They barely made it up the steps when the rain and wind came in with a fury. Richard heard the sound of thunder in the distance and quickly shut the windows they had left open.

He noticed her nervous expression. The rain started coming down in sheets, pounding on the windows. Richard tuned on the radio see if there were any weather updates being broadcast.

The announcer reported that a patrol led by Sergeant Holzinger crossed into Germany near the village of Stalzemburg.

"The troops have already made it from Paris to Germany, shouldn't be much longer." The house shook under their feet and a bright flash of lightning lit the room.

Carolyn closed her eyes and shook her head. The thunder continued to rattle everything. She could feel the force of the thunder outside and watched the lightning thrash across the room.

He opened a bottle of wine to drink with the pasta Carolyn was busy preparing. "This should take the edge off of the storm tonight."

"Radio is out." He tuned at the radio again, but he had lost the signal. "I'm going to call pop to make sure he got all the storm shutters closed okay." He picked up the receiver, tapped the cradle a few times and set the receiver back down. "Radio is out," he told her and sat down to eat. "Phone is out too."

"I think I will call tomorrow to ask about starting back at work. I think I'm better."

Richard leaned over to kiss her, "everything will be back to normal before we know it.

The thunder cracked outside. The torrents of rain beat down on the entire East Coast.

. . . .

Richard carried the last box into the house from their apartment in New York. He said his goodbyes the day before.

"Thanks guys for everything. A common bond has linked all of us for the past several years. Experiences that I will never forget and will shape the rest of my life. We have been a part of families bonding and growing, as well as death. Too many lives, soldiers, my baby and my parents."

It should be a time to celebrate, Japan had finally surrendered and the war was over. Church bells rang through the city that August night when President Truman announced the surrender. The world had finally found peace nearly four years after the enemy had bombed the Pacific fleet at anchor in Pearl Harbor.

Richard had counted up his points he earned both overseas, in combat, and his stateside duty to determine if he met the quota to leave the service. He decided to move to Martha's Vineyard when he received his discharge. His Army career was over and it was time to try to pick up the broken pieces and start over yet again. The bank his father had worked at offered Richard a job. They were well aware of his degree and his work in the service.

He set down the box and looked around the house, there were so many memories there even though they had been gone a year. It had been the hottest summer he could remember; he thought back to a year ago.

He had not thought to much when he was unable to reach his parents by phone that night. It really wasn't that uncommon. No one realized the enormity of the storm that was carried farther north than anticipated by the jet stream. It's powerful whirling action tore right up the coast line with heavy rain and damaging winds. He had never witnessed the high waves he heard accounts of that took his parents.

"What were they doing out there driving in that storm," he asked himself over and over.

He was finally getting through the tremendous grief of losing his son and then he was knocked down again with the news of his parents being found after the hurricane.

"One of the worst on record and dad was out there playing with his new camera." He still had not found the courage to have the film developed from the camera that was found still hanging around his father's neck. To see the last thing his parents looked at together. The last thing they were thinking about. Were they happy? Were they scared? Timothy underestimated the power of the hurricane.

The newspaper had several accounts about the storm from the island residents. The wind blowing bending the trees low and shaking the leaves from their branches. Flashes of lightning one after the other followed by thunder reverberating in a long continuous roar with no rest in between. It rained straight across, not just a little, but more like a wave crashing in from the ocean. It pounded and pounded like nothing they had seen before. The volumes of water running down the street was the color of the dirt, rushing in swells trying to escape back into the sea. Everything rattled and shook and if it wasn't tied down, it was lost. There were houses reduced to piles of rubble. He had heard the horrific stories and repeated them over and over in his sleep. The slim valley beyond the inlet saved the Moeller's house, and the cobblestone wall protected it from flooding. But it was not able to save its residents from what the storm threw at them outside of the protective confines.

He was given a hardship leave to take care his parent's affairs and clean up the little bit of damage there had been. How can you rebuild everything they have lost? He refused to lose hope! He had endured so much, but he had to keep going and move forward for the sake of his wellbeing and his wife's.

Friends of his parents stayed in the Moeller house while they rebuilt their own, it was the least Richard felt he could do to help and felt it was what his parents would have wanted.

"My parents moved in here when they were young and happy, I guess it is comforting that they went together." He moved through the room and wiped away the dust.

His mother was almost compulsively conscious of dust and would have never stood for the condition of the house. She was so proud of the house and the home she and her husband had nurtured their family in for so many years. Everything had order and discipline, the house and her son.

"Looks like mom was putting together another photo album with the pictures dad had been taking." The relics were now his along with the memories. Even the knitting needles and yarn that had been set aside by the chair. Yellow...

He opened the windows to allow some fresh air to flow through the room. The old smells flushed out by the smell of the flowers growing wild in the garden.

Carolyn moved quietly and watched her husband pacing through the house touching each memory of his mom and his dad. Their lives not yet finished, yet rudely interrupted.

Touching the lasting finger prints left by his parents. There was an odd quietude in sorting and packing what had been the life that his parents shared. They packed up what they needed to and moved the boxes to the attic and started to unpack their own new life.

The summer months were therapeutic for the young couple. They walked along the beach together and eventually started getting back to somewhat of a normal life. They enjoyed meeting for lunch at the small diner, watching a movie, and the occasional stroll on the beach.

Labor Day weekend was like a weeklong party atmosphere. The Japanese surrender was signed and troop ships were on the way home.

"There goes another one," Richard pointed out to the ship gliding up the eastern coastline.

"This is going to be a homecoming celebration to be remembered forever." Matthew and Helen came up for the weekend for a picnic on the beach.

The ships sailed along with all the fanfare trappings of a coronation. Fire boats trailed alongside, streaming fountains of water. The tug boats were whistling, sirens blowing, people on the shores waved and shouted!

"This is so exciting!" Helen's friend Hillary joined the group. She was deaf like Carolyn and Matthew and fit right in. She was intrigued by Carolyn's story escaping the violence in Europe and they quickly became close friends. She tapped Carolyn who was sitting on the blanket in the sand beside her.

"Aaaaah, I'm falling," Richard yelled, walking on his hands toward the women. He fell with a thud.

"Do you remember when I was on the tumbling team in high school?" Helen was signing to Matthew. Before he could answer she shared her accomplishments with the group. "I was always the one the coach would ask to perform and demonstrate the jumps. I have a medal from a competition we traveled to in Boston."

Helen jumped up from the blanket and attempted some kind of twisty floppy move and face planted in the sand. Everyone laughed.

"I guess I should have warmed up first, it has been a long time." She brushed herself off and plopped down beside Matthew for a consoling hug. "I was good," she pouted.

Hillary watched them, Helen demanding everyone's attention. It was annoying.

"Would you like to go shopping with me tomorrow? I would like to find a slip cover for the couch and Richard promised that I could buy some paints."

"I would love to see some of the things you have done." Hillary and Carolyn were signing so fast hardly anyone else could follow their conversation.

"Carolyn does draw very nicely." Helen picked out a few of the words. "I've seen them. She has drawings of her hands that she drew for Richard - little messages for him."

Hillary turned back to Carolyn and nodded with approval.

"That's how she told him that she was going to have a baby!" Helen tapped at Hillary to get her attention back.

"You're going to have a baby?" Hillary clapped with excitement.

"No," Carolyn looked away. It still hurt to think about the little boy that she never got to hold.

"She lost the..."

"Stop!" Matthew yelled using his voice and slapped his hands down on the other. "You don't have to bring that up. Just stop it."

"How dare you yell at me." Helen reached for her bag and started stuffing her towel into it. She put on her hat and stood up.

"Take me home now! I won't have you embarrassing me." She was tearing up and her face was turning bright red.

"Me embarrass you? You do nothing but butt into every conversation whether it involves you or not. You talk incessantly." He picked up their blanket and started to head after her. Her heals kicking up sand with each vehement step toward the car.

"Wait," Richard jumped up scattering sand all over trying to catch Matthew's attention. "Don't forget, nine o'clock sharp tomorrow morning."

"I'll be there, thanks."

"Is she always like that?"

"Yes. She signs pretty good so it is hard to ignore her. She is always right up in my face. I don't like it, but she is nice enough."

"I don't know how he puts up with her."

"I think she is insecure and just begging for attention." Richard sat back down beside Carolyn. "Besides, that means more of your sandwiches for me." He laughed and took a bite of one of the cucumber sandwiches.

"Fresh from the garden."

"Are you sure Helen didn't grow them with her own Midas touch?"

"You are naughty," he pointed out to their new friend. "But I love you both."

They stayed on the beach to watch the sunset and fireworks celebrating a world finally without war and a new friendship.

Richard was already in bed when Carolyn came out of the bathroom. She had taken extra time in the shower to get all of the sand and salt from the ocean out of her hair. She walked over to the mirror in her towel and started running a brush through the wet strands.

"I miss you," he walked up behind her and kissed her neck.

She could see his reflection in the mirror. "I'm sorry I have not been a good wife to you."

Since losing the baby, the thought of making love was not easy. He hadn't pushed the subject and even when they did make love, it wasn't as intimate as most young couples would expect. Carolyn did as she felt she was obligated to do.

"Stop that. It isn't true. You are a great wife."

"I'm scared of getting pregnant again. We have both lost so much, it is difficult."

"I know," he took the brush and ran it through her hair for her.

"I do need you. I want you to be happy."

"I need you too."

She turned to face her husband and unhooked the corner of her towel and let it drop to the floor.

He picked her up and moved to the bed that they had picked out together just weeks ago. They moved his parent's big poster bed to the room that used to be his.

He could feel goose pimples on her skin under his fingers. He laid down beside her running his fingers up and down, exploring the body that he had longed for so much.

"Slow," she signed. She had an intense desire that she had held back for so long from fear. She owed it to her husband to be the partner she promised to be. She tucked away the pain.

He ran his hands on the flesh still damp from the shower. His fingertips rounded her hips and detoured around her navel.

Her skin tingled and her body ached. She could feel her heart beating hungrily in her chest, and the warmth from his hands. She could feel his heat as he moved on top of her. He lifted her slightly positioning her head on the pillow and moved his lips from one side to the other, touching and tasting. Finally, he drew her in and met her body moving like the waves coming in to the shore.

Carolyn woke to an empty bed; Richard was careful not to move around too much and wake her. She reached over to feel if his pillow was still warm. She rolled back over to get up and noticed spots of blood on her side of the bed. She got up, dressed, and took the bedding down to the washer.

"Am I too early?" Hillary blinked the lights to get Carolyn's attention.

"No, come on in. I just slept in a little." She glowed like she hadn't in a long time.

"Is Dickey here?"

"He is working," she smiled at the name. Hillary seemed to enjoy applying her own nickname to everyone. "He works at the bank where his father worked. Matthew has an appointment there today to see about a job."

"I've been here before actually, but I doubt he remembers. My mom brought me with her once when I was little, she was picking up some mending from his mother. He just stared at me while I stood there. I didn't even realize who he was until just now when I walked in."

Carolyn handed her a cup of coffee. "What was he like when he was little."

"Like any other boy, I guess. I really didn't know him and I was only here a few times. Not much had changed from what she recalled. "I do remember that he was pretty dirty. He had just come home and was still holding a baseball glove."

"I never really thought about him growing up here." She looked around and pictured a grubby little boy standing there. It could have been their little boy standing there with a glove and a bat just in from a game with the neighborhood kids.

"It is a nice place to grow up. There are a lot of people here like us, you know deaf. So, I never felt 'different'. Not like I do when I go to the city with my mom. I feel like people think I have a disease or something. What was it like to grow up in Paris? How exciting it must have been to grow up in such a beautiful place."

"Exciting until the German army marched in."

"Did you see them?" Hillary sat forward in her chair

"Too much of them. And they would sit at our cafes like they belonged. Like they were on holiday. It was sickening."

"They sat there and ate? I always pictured them like in the newspaper."

"I remember one morning waking up and there were a lot of them. And German flags hanging all over the streets. We had to move carefully, my grandmother told me to be nice and not to make them angry."

"Where is your grandmother?"

"She passed away. My parents, my brother, they are all gone now. My grandmother had the most outrageous costumes that she would let me dress up in. She was wonderful."

"So, you moved in with your grandmother when your parents passed away."

"After the bombing." She opened up to Hillary and shared details that she had never before been able to pull from the terrible memories. "I remember mama shaking me from my sleep, she was frightened, I could tell from her face. She handed me blankets and signed for me to go down to the shelter. Hurry she told me, hurry!"

Hillary grabbed the coffee pot from the stove and refilled both of their cups, as Carolyn continued.

"I remember running down the steps and our neighbor holding the door open as we passed through. I knew the bombs were coming, the stone walls shook and dust filled the room and everything went black just as I found an empty place on the floor. There was more shaking and I felt someone fall on my feet. I pulled my knees up to my chest and prayed for it to end, but the walls kept shaking. It was hard to breathe from all the dust. I must have fallen asleep at some point or passed out; I don't know which. But I thought someone lit a candle, but it was the sunlight shining through where the building used to be. It was gone. It was all gone."

"How scary! And your family?"

"I didn't know if they made it into the shelter or not. There wasn't much light, but enough to see a lot of people laying around. I didn't know if they were alive or dead, I couldn't see everything. I felt my way along the walls, tripping over people. I remember crying and thinking the door was here, there has to be a door here. But there was no door, no door knob, just chunks of stone and beams of splintered wood. I remember clawing at the concrete trying to move the heavy blocks. I remembered the stairs being there so I crawled through a gap and tried to work my way up, it was so hard to see and I kept coughing from the dirt and realized it was also smoke. I shut my eyes and kept moving, trusted my memory of what the stairway used to look like. I told myself that if I kept reaching out that my father would grab onto my hand and pull me out."

"How did you finally get out?" Hillary would have held her hands if it wouldn't have prevented them from being able to speak to one another.

"I still had my eyes closed, they burned if I opened them. I prayed to myself for someone to find us. Then I felt someone take my hand and pull me out of the rubble. I waited in the street for hours while they pulled out one after another hoping my mother and father would be the next to be saved, but they never came. I even looked at the bodies that they covered with blankets before their faces were hidden."

"I've read a lot of stories about the bombings and stories about the soldiers. I just can't imagine going through that."

"I remembered standing and watching, my head was spinning and everything got blurry, I couldn't focus. I woke up in the hospital and that is when they told me my parents were found... dead. I was a war orphan."

"Then you went to live with your grandmother." Hillary was drying her eyes.

"She lived farther in the city; it was safer there. I could look out the window of my new room and see the Eiffel Tower. It is taller than all the buildings in New York."

"Do you think you will ever go back?"

"Richard and I have talked about it, but we haven't made any plans yet. We didn't want to until the war ended."

"I lost both of my brothers, somewhere in France. I would like to go over sometime and try to find their graves."

"I hope we never have to live through anything like that again. Do you know where they were?"

"My oldest brother was in Africa and later was transferred to France after the invasion last year. My younger brother was lost somewhere between Normandy and Paris. I have his last letter; I've read it a hundred times. He said he was writing from a foxhole and living in mud. He said he felt like he was ingesting more mud than food. He described the continuous flow of planes overhead, but said the countryside was beautiful. He was adamant that he was going to come back and enjoy Paris when the war was over. Russell had been training but he didn't say for what but he made it sound like something big. I'm assuming it was for D-Day because we never heard from him again."

"I guess we have a lot in common." Both women had already experienced too much grief in their young lives.

"I remember the soldiers walking up to the house. My mom couldn't even go to the door, she knew. It was all very official; they said the President regretted to inform her that her son was killed in action. I read the letter later after mother left it laying on the sideboard. I will never forget the incredible pain I felt when I realized that I would never see my brother again. She still has the flag with the two gold stars hanging in the window."

"The stars for your brothers."

Hillary shook her head.

"You should go over when we go, I may be able to help you get around. But, I'm sure a lot has changed since I left."

"We will go shopping and buy fancy French dresses!"

"Wait until you see the pretty little boutiques, mama and I would go and look at the beautiful dresses. Grandmother bought as many as she could after I came home to her. I had no clothes when I left the hospital."

"Speaking of shopping, we should go if we are going to get out."

"I'm hungry too," Carolyn ran her fingers down her neck.

"I saw one of the crab boats coming in, I haven't had a crab sandwich in a while."

Carolyn stepped into Hillary's car and grabbed the door to close it. She felt a pull on her side and winced.

"You okay?" Hillary was watching.

"I'm fine. I think I pulled a muscle while running around on the beach yesterday."

"That will definitely make you sore." She backed out of the driveway. "I don't know how much you have been able to get out and see since you moved here, but I'm going to take you to my favorite place."

Ten minutes later Hillary proved to be right. It was the cutest little shop Carolyn had seen.

"When is the last time you bought silk stockings?"

"I haven't had a pair since I came to America. I never could spend the money."

"Didn't you say that your grandmother left everything to you?"

"Yes, but it wasn't until recently that I received the money. It was tied up in the bank in France and it was too difficult to get the money over here."

"Have you ever seen one of her movies?"

"No, and I think it was because my mother never allowed my father to talk about them."

"That's funny. What kind of character do you think she was playing?"

"She always talked about dancing, so I assumed it was some kind of burlesque, you know like at Moulin Rouge."

"The what?"

"It's a cabaret in Paris. The women dance in these slight outfits dancing the can-can."

"Sounds simply wicked." Hillary held up a piece of lingerie and giggled making a throaty sound. "Maybe you should do a little can-can in this."

"No!" Carolyn mashed her fingers together; her eyes open wide. "We haven't been close to often since the baby died."

"No better reason then." Hillary handed the silky garment to her. "It's naughty, but fun..."

"What do you know about that?"

"Dreaming and waiting for my prince charming I guess. It's fun to feel like a woman."

"I don't know that I would ever wear this," Carolyn blushed.

"Not for long at least!"

Carolyn smiled a nervous smile and pretended to admire the teddy.

"Do you think you will have more children?" She sensed it was a difficult topic for Carolyn.

"Someday perhaps. Richard has been so patient with me."

"He's a good man."

"Yes," she nodded with her hand. "He is everything you could ever want in a man."

"I am simply ravenous, let's go eat." Hillary paid for her stockings and didn't pressure Carolyn about buying anything.

They walked down the pier to a quaint little diner and sat at one of the wooden tables outside along the railing. The enjoyed Lobster rolls, and egg salad and chips.

"This is a treat. Thank you for coming out with me today. It will be nice for life to get back to normal."

"This is so good." Carolyn licked the buttery sauce from her fingers.

They sat back and finished a glass of local wine. Different crafts sailed past, the occasional sailboat and skiff. A few tied up to the pier and joined the others enjoying the food and excellent weather.

Carolyn invited Hillary to stay over and to help make dinner while waiting for Richard to come home.

They are tossing flour at each other and running around the kitchen when he walks in the door. He stands and watches the two women and notices the half empty bottle of wine on the counter.

"Hi" Carolyn waves and wipes her hands on her apron. She gives her husband a kiss and leaves a white floured hand print on his chin where she held it.

"Lynnie is showing me how to make Hominy pie." Hillary hands him a glass of wine and raises her glass to toast him. "I don't really know what it is, but it's a lot of fun."

"I can see that." He raises his eyebrows to his wife.

"We have had the most fabulous day." She is pushing her hands into the air as she signs.

"It is good to see you so happy." He opens the oven to inspect the potato and leek vegetable pie. "Smells good. I hope it tastes good because I have a feeling you were a bit distracted."

"When we go to Paris, I want Hillary to come with us. Both of her brothers are buried somewhere in France, and we thought we could find them."

"I'm sorry about your brothers," too often those word had been spoken. Too many letters, and too many telegrams stating the demise of another soldier. He sat down at the table hoping the two women would follow his lead and sit down as well.

"Thanks," it was sobering to think that she may actually go to Europe some day and find her brothers' final resting spots.

"I want to climb the steps in the Arc de Triomphe, and ride the elevator to the top of the Eiffel Tower. We can watch the sunset down the Champs-Elysees. I want to show you where grandmother lived and where my house stood, maybe leave some flowers for my family."

"That would be nice." Richard agreed. Carolyn tended to sink into despair when she got onto the subject of home, he needed to change the subject before the gaiety from the wine changed to depression. "So, what did you two do today?" He took another sip of his wine.

"We went to all the little shops," Hillary looked at Carolyn and smirked. "Even the naughty one."

"Hillary, stop!" She signed the symbol for Hillary's name and then chopped her right hand onto her left.

Richard was intrigued by this new information. "Tell me more."

"Dinner is ready and we don't have time to talk about the foolishness from this afternoon." She was having doubts about having gone back into the boutique and picking out one of the more modest nightgowns than what Hillary thought she should have bought.

"I'll show you later, maybe." There was a burst of happiness in her heart wanting to resume a normal married life.

The threesome talked for hours until Richard had to call it a night. "I have to get up early in the morning."

Hillary stretched her legs and stood up with a wide yawn. "Thank you for a great day and a very nice evening." She kissed them both on the cheek and winked at Carolyn. "Goodnight Lynnie, night Dickey."

"Goodnight."

"I like the Lynnie nickname, but I don't think I like the Dickey thing."

"She is so nice and so much fun."

"It is nice to see you so happy. Now, let's see what you bought on your shopping trip."

Hillary was right, it didn't stay on long!

CHAPTER 14 LEGACY

THE MONTHS FLEW BY. If Carolyn wasn't with Hillary running errands or working with one group or another, she found joy in drawing or painting for endless hours in the sunlit room. There were so many fun and exciting pieces of their life to share, filled in by the senseless and mundane things. Life was perfect and nothing could change how happy they were.

It was early spring, Carolyn's favorite time of the year. She loved how the winter transformed into spring unlike the weather in Paris that seemed to exude clouds and rain more often than not. The smell of the island's beauty, not just the wild dahlias and zinnias; but also, the variety of sunflowers growing beyond the perimeter of their property mixed with the salty air.

For some time now she had felt the pull in her side. It was time to tell him what she expected.

"I think I want to decorate the room at the top of the stairs."

"Okay...?" He didn't think much of the statement. "What do you have in mind? How about we set up your easel and paints so you don't have to be down here with all the distractions?"

"I had something more youthful in mind, maybe yellow."

"Yellow?" He set down his coffee and looked more closely at his wife. "Are you trying to tell me something?"

"I haven't had my monthly cycle in almost two months, so I must be pregnant." She smiled as he took her in her arms and spun her around. Carolyn tapped his shoulder for him to stop as the action was causing her pain. "I have been sick in the mornings, and tender," she pointed to her belly.

"This is great! Right? Are you happy about this?"

"I am very happy," she brushed her open palm up on her chest.

"I want you to see the doctor. I want to make sure that you take it easy and get plenty of rest."

"I'm fine, but yes, I will go to the doctor."

"I will call and make an appointment for you and I will see about going in with you." He takes her hand and kisses her fingers and catches a glimpse of his watch. "I have to get to work. Matthew and I have a meeting with some of the board members, I will see you later."

"Do you mind if I tell Hillary? I wanted to tell you first, but she is coming over later and…"

"You share the news with her. She is going to be just as excited as we are. I guess I can tell Matthew too."

Hillary ran up the stairs after she finished hugging her friend. "This is so exciting, a baby! We can paint the room and start decorating. There are so many decisions to make. Baby ducks, I love baby ducks."

"What if something happens again." Her heart was hammering. Carolyn was cautiously thrilled.

"You can't think like that. Everything is going to be fine. I'm even going to ask Helen to help me plan a baby shower."

"You and Helen? I thought she drove you crazy."

"She does, but I just won't look at her and I won't know when she is talking."

Carolyn grinned. Hillary had a much stronger personality than she did, but came across more playful and lighthearted than forceful.

"We are going to go inland and shop in Boston. We will make a day of it!"

"I'm tired out just thinking about it." She felt the catch in her side that had been bothering her.

"Baby kick already?"

"Hardly. It is just my body starting to adjust for the baby."

"I'm too selfish to have a baby. Just think what it would do to my figure!"

"You will make a wonderful mother someday. I think we should find you someone."

"That's what I need. A pregnant lady looking for a man for me. Unless he's a doctor. I think you are on to something there. Mrs. Doctor Somebody."

"What about Mrs. Marin?"

"What about her?"

"She's nice, and if she's nice I'm sure her son is too."

"Only that her son is ten years older than me, fat and bald."

"But nice!"

They started a sketch of what they planned to do to the nursery. Carolyn was going to show Richard before they started their shopping.

"The baby can call my Auntie Hilly. What do you think?" There has to be an easy sign for the baby to learn my name. She circled her fist at her jaw line, but instead of holding out her thumb she held out her two fingers for the letter "H".

"The baby will need an aunt, or a God Mother - and I think you are perfect for the job."

A week passed and Richard was taking Carolyn to the doctor who had been on holiday, but took the couple in as soon as he returned.

He asked all of the pertinent questions that they had been asked the last time. The doctor poked and prodded, measured her belly and wrote down his observations.

After Carolyn was dressed, they all met in the doctor's office.

"Based on your body changes and from what you've told me, I'd speculate that you are about three months pregnant" He looked right at Carolyn so that she could read his lips and understand what he was telling them.

Richard was counting out the months and trying to come up with an approximate due date. "You think September?"

"Possibly. It is too early to hear the baby's heart sounds, and I didn't detect any fetal movements, but it is early yet. I gave her a pregnancy test, but even that will take several days until we know for sure."

"But you think that everything adds up to Carolyn being pregnant." Richard wanted to know for sure, and reassurance that the baby was going to be fine this time.

Carolyn watched the conversation; she wasn't convinced from the doctor's expressions that he had concluded the diagnosis.

"Does she smoke?"

They both shook their heads, no.

"Good. There is no reason to believe that moderation would hurt. Your nerves shouldn't be upset during this time, calm and sweet temperament." He wrote out a note and raised his head to address them again.

"I'm not entirely sure, but ... it may be from the miscarriage, but something just doesn't feel right. I've written down the name of a specialist in Boston that I want you two to go see."

"Is something wrong with the baby?" Carolyn was signing anxiously while Richard translated to the doctor.

"I don't know. That is why I want you to go to this appointment. They have equipment that can help to determine what it is I'm seeing."

Carolyn and Hillary spent the following week flipping through catalogs for everything they needed for the baby's room.

Carolyn grew increasingly nervous as they crossed downtown looking for the address they were given. Richard reassured her and told her that the doctor was just being cautious. He would always be there and never let her down.

A nurse in a white dress calls her name. Richard tapped her arm and pointed out that it was her turn to see the doctor.

"She'll be fine, you just wait here and I will have her back out shortly."

"Everything will be okay," she signed back. "Don't worry."

The door closed behind her and he was left in the waiting room worried that her optimism may be misplaced.

A few minutes turned into eternity. He flipped through a LIFE magazine, paced by the window, and checked his watch to make sure it wasn't running fast. It was the longest hour ever, finally the nurse came out to see him.

"The doctor would like to speak to you. Your wife is already waiting in his office." She escorted him down the hall. The sterile smell made him nauseous, or was it the fear that maybe something was wrong.

"Mr. Moeller." The doctor rose from behind the desk and took Richard's hand. "Please sit," he motioned him to the empty chair beside Carolyn. "I don't know how much Dr. Parker discussed with you, but there is an abnormality to your wife's cervix."

"I don't remember," Richard stammered. He looked at Carolyn who appeared unemotional. Maybe they had not said anything to her yet.

"I wouldn't get alarmed just yet. The cervix..." he looked to make sure Richard was following what he was saying. "It should be soft and high right now. Carolyn's..." he turned to her. "Are you understanding me okay?"

"Yes," she smiled a fragile smile and nodded.

"Carolyn's cervix is hard or rigid as we describe it. And she has reported pain and bleeding during intercourse."

Richard looked to her in disbelief and guilt from feeling like he had hurt her. He felt the heat build on his face and the strain of holding back his tears. 'Be strong,' he told himself and took her hand and squeezed ever so slightly.

"I ran some tests; some will take longer than others for the results. I have the results from the pregnancy test Dr. Parker ran, I'm sorry, but you are not pregnant."

She followed his words exactly, they caught in her throat and she turned a faint-hearted glance to her husband. "I'm sorry," she circled her fist around her stomach.

"You have nothing to be sorry about."

"He's right," the doctor tried to reassure them. "No one can predict these things, and we don't even know for sure what is going on yet. For now, I want you to go home and rest."

"Is there anything special we should be doing?"

"Not now," he answered Richard's question. "When I get the test results back, I will call you. Whatever is causing the problems, rest is the best thing for now."

• • • •

They had just finished dinner two days later when the phone rang. Carolyn was laying on the couch reading and looked up and smiled when she saw him go over and pick up the phone.

"Mr. Moeller, it's Doctor Macklin."

"Do you have the results back?"

"Yes, and I wanted to know if you would like to come back to my office so we can discuss the reports."

Richard looked at Carolyn and then back to the phone, "sure, when would you like to see us?"

"Tomorrow morning. I have cleared my schedule for you."

"Okay, we'll be there. And thanks for calling." He set the received down and tried to put on a smile before going back into the living room.

Carolyn looked at him with wide eyes and raised eyebrows. She raised her hand and twisted her three fingers in a "W" and closed her hand. "What?"

"That was the doctor, he wants to see us tomorrow." He tried to act nonchalant and unmoved by the hurried sound in the doctor's voice.

Richard tried to think positive and remain supportive for Carolyn. He didn't want to see her worry. He readied himself for the news, but why did it have to be bad news. Some medicine and she'd be fine. He was worrying for no reason at all. If they couldn't have children, they could eventually adopt. There were thousands of orphans that came over from Europe. What a great idea! A baby, or a toddler from France, it was perfect.

Richard has every scenario in his head that he can imagine and rehearsed how he would tell Carolyn that everything was okay.

"She apparently has experienced abnormal bleeding for some time now along with pain in her side. Based on her past, her failure to report this was either governed by fear or ignorance. In either case, the delay in getting treatment increases the challenge ahead of you."

"Cancer? Are you sure? She really thought she was pregnant." He held his breath. If he could just breathe everything was going to go back to normal. He has to calm down, just breathe!

"I'm sorry. We can try surgery, but honestly, I think it has spread too far. Her lymph nodes in her neck and groin area are swollen. It is probably what took the baby last year and has been growing inside her for years."

He can't hold back the tears any more. How is it that she is so strong? The news that he had been dreading. He gazes at Carolyn.

She knew somewhere in her heart that it wasn't going to be good news. The pain for months and all the little signs that she ignored. She winced when she read the doctors lips. It seemed so cruel after all she had already been through. Everything she loved was always taken away.

Doctor Macklin passes a sympathetic exchange. He explains what he can do and their options.

• • • •

Carolyn continues to draw and paint when she has the strength, her wonderful memories. She was making a pictorial memoir of her own deterioration. She has always been strong. She survived the bombed-out ruins of her home, survived crossing the Atlantic among the U-boats just waiting to take out any threat, military or civilian. On some of the drawings, she would write a story on the back about the picture and the things she endured in her short lifetime. Richard read the stories at night as he sat by her side watching her sleep.

On the back of a simple pencil drawing of a forest, she wrote about escaping Paris. The story grew in length, so she eventually added more illustrations and shared her memories on a Chief tablet.

"My grandmother woke me at night and told me it was time to go. I knew where I was to be going, but did not know how. I had never seen the man waiting for me to climb aboard the horse drawn cart before. He covered me in a thick wool blanket, 'don't move' I watched his lips. The cart bumped as it crossed over the cobblestone streets and then to the wooded area. We must have been moving south because the ride became very rough and to go north would have been too dangerous. I eventually fell asleep and woke in the morning when we reached a farm house. I could smell eggs and rashers which made my stomach rumble. There was a Jewish girl with us, I can't remember her name but she was very polite and tried to communicate with me. She loved to brush my hair. I taught her how to finger spell, and after the two weeks hiding out, she was doing very well. Eventually, I was handed a cloth sack with my papers and money my grandmother had sent to pay for my passage. We headed out again in a wagon with hay and sacks to hide us."

Richard flipped through the folder of pictures that she had been assembling in her times of clarity. It seemed as if she were sleeping more and more lately. He admired the picture of the trees in the distant; tiny specs compared to the wood planks they were obstructed by.

"I would watch the country side pass by in the sliver of a gap between the boards on the side of the wagon. Occasionally, I would watch through a large knot hole that had been punched out. The constant bouncing wore sores on my skin, I wanted so badly to move about but was warned not to. I could feel the wagon slowing its pace and then came to a stop. I thought I was going to burst I needed to relieve myself - instead I froze. I realized why the others were not moving. They heard what I could only see. A uniform. I could clearly see the insignia on his tunic, a German Soldier. It was different from those I had seen in Paris, but there was a German soldier so close that he could possibly feel how quickly I was breathing. I tried to hold my breath in. I imagined him reaching in and pulling me out. I had read what the retched soldiers would do to young women, I was in my latter teens and would surely be subjected to their cruelty. I watched his mud-covered boots step back. I filled my lungs back with air when we started to move again, leaving behind several more pairs of boots and the soldiers oblivious to the passengers in my wagon."

Richard picked up the drawing that she had been working on earlier. Although unfinished, he could tell that it was the railing of a ship. Most likely the ship she sailed on to America. She didn't talk about the experience often, maybe that is why she was doing this now; to document what she and thousands of others experienced trying to escape to safety. She had mentioned a few times that she crossed on a cruise ship and could see the other ships escorting them from the railing. She spent the majority of her time tending to the refugee children traveling without their parents. She ripped the offensive yellow star from their clothing. There were plenty of hugs and cuddles to go around.

She decided that she wanted to stay in the guest room, "you need your rest also. I rest better when I am not worried about waking you up."

"If that is where you are the most comfortable."

"Think of it as my grandmother's magic bed, it looks just like it. It will take care of me just like her bed protected me."

He stayed with her as much as he could. Hillary was at the house constantly helping with whatever Carolyn needed.

Hillary's heart scolded her for not saying something about Lynnie's pains. Why had she not been honest with her or herself? Hillary sat with her on the back patio, pulled the wrap up to cover her friend's legs.

Carolyn smiled, her face brightened and she patted her friend's hand. "You are a good friend," she signed.

"That's because I love you."

"Will you keep an eye on Richard for me? I want him to be happy."

"He loves you too and you had better keep your eyes on him. You just keep strong. I'm not giving up on you."

"Promise to take care of him when I'm gone. He doesn't have anyone else."

"I promise. Now, it's time to get you back inside so we can make dinner. Let's get this stuff inside." She took the picture that Lynnie was working on and set it aside and eventually moved it upstairs inside the closet with the easel.

The picture was a finger pointing upward. She smudged the charcoal creating a swirling motion on the finger.

"Forever."

"Yes, my love for you and Richard both - forever."

• • • •

Eventually, the pain was too intense to follow her usual household routine with comfort or to walk a good distance with ease. The doctor prescribed bed rest, accompanied with local treatments including a hot water bottle. Richard gave her the prescribed Morphine when she needed it. She was losing weight, looking pinched and worn. She was pale and found it difficult to eat. He brought her tea and broth, but as time went on, she continued to become gaunt and her eyes visibly sank deeper into their sockets.

He dropped to his knees beside her bed and prayed. The tears flowed down his cheeks and dripped onto the white sheet. "Please, take her pain away. She has suffered so much pain in her life, just don't make her suffer." He concentrated on her breathing and touched her cool skin. He suddenly felt something inside that was comforting. He felt different, she was happy...

Richard looked up at his wife. She stroked the side of his face wiping away his tears.

"I love you," she held her three fingers out to him.

He watched as a warm glow seemed to shroud her. Her pain and sadness fading. He listened as her breathing slowed. Richard crawled up beside her to feel her heart beat and her final breath as she drew it in, quietly and peacefully she breathed out.

• • • •

Richard sat in the empty room starring at the framed picture, a gift from his wife expressing her love for him. He had been slowly packing up her things in the weeks that had gone by since he buried his wife.

Someone was knocking on the door. He ignored it. They knocked again.

Richard steadied himself, walked over and opened the door.

"Hi," the younger man waved. "Do you sign? I'm sorry, it has been so long since I have used my hands to talk."

"I can hear you, what can I do for you?" He was slightly irritated for having been interrupted in his grief.

"Are you Richard Moeller?"

"Yes?" He eyed the stranger with the unusual accent.

"Are you Carolyn Lagaisse, I mean Moeller's husband?"

"Yes, what is this about?"

"I'm Jene Lagaisse."

Richard stood not understanding the significance to the man or to what he was saying."

"I'm Carolyn's brother."

"Lynnie? Oh no!"

"I'm sorry?" He didn't understand the reaction. "Are you Richard Moeller?"

"Yes, please come in." He stepped aside and let the male version of his wife into their home. He had the same hair and piercing eyes.

"Is she here," he smiled. "It has been so long, I'm sure this may be a shock to her. I didn't know where she was for so long, and then I sailed to America to inquire at the school grandmother sent her to. I saw one of her paintings hanging in the hall and asked about the picture. The professor told me that she painted the picture from her window looking out to the ocean."

"She passed away, just recently. I'm sorry."

"I'm too late."

"She never knew you were alive. She assumed you died with your parents."

"I was in the hospital for a long time. I was unconscious for months and when I did wake up, it took a long time for me to be able to remember anything."

"She would have looked for you had she known."

"It looks just like the picture," he moved to the window looking down to the inlet and out to the ocean.

"She drew and painted a lot. Can I show you some?" He took his brother-in-law upstairs where he kept the majority of her paintings and drawings. He opened the door, he could feel her around him, comforting him. The coolness when he entered her room, the cool touch on the side of his face. It was difficult not to glimpse at the empty bed and expect to see her there. His unease seemed to vanish every time he felt her.

Richard moved to allow Jene into the room, he looked and wondered if he could feel her as well. How would she have reacted to learn that her brother had been alive all along.

"She used to draw all the time when we were kids. I'm sure the sketch books and papers were all destroyed during the bombings."

Richard opened the closet door to pull out some of the pictures that were rolled up. He moved her easel aside and notice a canvas that he did not recognize. He didn't know when she drew the picture, it was her last. Her signature drawing of her hand; a finger pointing skyward. The shading made it appear that her finger was making a swirling motion. "Forever"

"She never knew she left me a gift of family."

"She knows." Jene said.

Chapter 15 tRISH

• • • •

There was a light wind sweeping in from the ocean, blowing through her hair. The pine trees dripping from the light rain that fell. It was a perfect day to work on cleaning the attic, the combination of Kevin's things, her boxes and the few remaining things from the Moeller's. Trish sat on the back step with the old leather album resting on her knees, dusted off the cover and flipped through the pages she had been through so many times years ago. The sun reflecting through her glass onto a picture of a couple drew her eye to the image. The woman was holding a baby on the porch of the house. This house. "Kevin, look at this!"

Trish marched up to the retirement home, flung the door open and walked in the room, Ralph and Carol were already in a rousing game of Chinese Checkers.

"Why didn't you tell me?!" Trish tapped her fingers forming a "Y" on her forehead and quickly moved her hands to her hips, glaring at Hillary.

"I knew you would figure it out..." Hillary smiled at her. "We turned to each other for comfort after she died and ended up loving each other. Your story was about Lynnie, not me."

ABOUT THE AUTHOR

• • • •

DOREY RASMUSSEN PETTY is the author of My Hands Have Something To Say, available on AMAZON in paperback and KINDLE editions. Inspired by her deaf niece and Dorey's own hearing disability, she hopes to expose others to the beauty of Sign Language. Dorey and her husband live in Texas and share her two boys, his daughter and son, and four amazing grandchildren (Troy, AJ, Haylee, and Harrison).

Don't miss out!

Visit the website below and you can sign up to receive emails whenever Dorey Rasmussen publishes a new book. There's no charge and no obligation.

https://books2read.com/r/B-A-TKTPB-BDDOD

BOOKS2READ

Connecting independent readers to independent writers.

Also by Dorey Rasmussen

My Hands Have Something To Say
Signs of Silence

Standalone
My Hands Have Something To Say